Nothing
But
Drama

Nothing
But
Drama

ReShonda Tate Billingsley

Pocket Books

New York   London   Toronto   Sydney

POCKET BOOKS, a division of Simon & Schuster, Inc.
1230 Avenue of the Americas, New York, NY 10020

ISBN-13: 978-1-4165-2560-8
ISBN-10:   1-4165-2560-2

This Pocket Books trade paperback edition November 2006

10 9 8 7 6 5 4 3 2 1

Manufactured in the United States of America

For information regarding special discounts for bulk purchases,
please contact Simon & Schuster Special Sales at 1-800-456-6798
or business@simonandschuster.com.

For Mya and Morgan,
something to make you proud.

Acknowledgments

I have to start off giving thanks to God for gracing me with the talent to tell stories people are interested in.

And, of course, my beautiful baby girls—Mya Simone and Morgan Camille. You're still not old enough to read and understand these words. But when you are, understand that you were the driving force behind what I do. This book is my way of saying thank you for sharing your mommy with the world with very few tears or complaints. To my husband, Miron, who does what few men can do— let me shine with few complaints. I wouldn't be where I am without your love and support.

To my mother, Nancy, thank you for nurturing my talent. I hope this book makes you proud. And don't worry: all the drama my characters in this story have with their mamas—none of it was drawn from you. To my wonderful sister-slash-personal assistant, who was quick to tell me I wasn't as hip as I thought I was (I'm sorry, but I still know people who say "da bomb"). Thanks for all you do, especially answering my endless "is this cool to say" questions.

My ace, boon coon (do they still say that, Tanisha?), Pat Tucker Wilson. Girl, I could spend the next ten pages thanking you for all you've done for me . . . the hours and hours of conversations. You keeping me grounded and sane with everything from the TV station to the literary industry. There are very few people in this world I know I can call at the drop of a dime about anything. You're one of them. I told you your time was coming. Now do your thang.

To Jihad, thanks for the endless feedback and teaching me to know that I don't know. Keep your head up and keep trying to educate through your writing. It's going to pay off.

To my wonderful, spectacular, fabulous, phenomenal, dynamic editor, Selena James (can you tell I have mad love for her?). Thank you so much for nurturing me on this literary journey and listening with a straight face as I brainstorm endless ideas that sometimes I know have you wanting to say, "Get real." To Louise Burke, Melissa Gramstad, Brigitte Smith, and everyone else at Pocket Books, thank you for believing in my work. The sky's the limit.

And you know I have to give a huge, huge thanks to my agent, Sara Camilli, who is always looking out for me and believed in me way back when.

Thanks so much to all the wonderful members of my teen advisory board—you guys are "da bomb."

Thanks also to the authors who never hesitate to help a sister out: Victoria Christopher Murray, Nina Foxx, Norma Jarrett, Jacquelin Thomas (you gotta check out her inspirational teen books as well), Sheila Dansby Harvey, Harold Turley, James Guittard, Carl Weber, and Zane and the Strebor Family.

Now, let me get to the part that I know is going to get me in trouble because I know I'll leave someone out. But here goes . . .

Thanks so much, as always, to my sorors in Alpha Kappa Alpha Sorority, Inc., especially the Houston Area Chapters, including my own—Mu Kappa Omega. My girls Jaimi Canady, Raquelle Lewis, Kim Wright, Clemelia Richardson, Finisha Waits, Beverly Davis, and Trina McReynolds.

Also thanks to Deidre Lodrig, Angie Pickett Henderson, Saki Indakwa, my coworkers at Fox 26 News, and all my other friends and family. (There, that covers everyone I know.)

Thanks to the schools and churches that have already had me out and allowed me to do what I do best—inspire and motivate young people; especially Contemporary Learning Center, Madison High School (my high school), Christa McAuliffe Middle School, Klentzman Intermediate, Alief Hastings, St. Luke's Baptist Church (and my pastor, Harvey Walker), Brentwood, Brookhollow, Friendship West, New Birth, Mt. Horeb and Higher Dimensions Baptist Churches, as well as Windsor Village United Methodist Church.

Thanks also to all the book clubs and book stores that have shown me mad, mad love. Hopefully, you'll spread the word about the teen books like you have my adult novels. Let's get young people reading!

And thank you, hopefully, my new reader. You no longer have to sneak and read something your parents don't want you to read, or force your way through a book they want you to read. It's my hope that this is a happy medium you all will come to love.

Look for my next books, *Blessings in Disguise* and *With Friends Like These,* as Camille, Alexis, Jasmine, and Angel continue to bring you stories that will entertain and inspire.

Until then, drop me a line and let me know what you think of the books.

Thanks for the love.

Peace.

Nothing
But
Drama

Camille

If my mother caught me, it would be all over.

I could see it now. All my friends, crying their eyes out. Even the haters would come out, pretending the world wouldn't be the same without me in it. Everyone would talk about what a shame it was that I had to go so soon. Yep, I had played out all the possibilities in my mind.

I wiped the sweat that was trickling down the side of my face. I wasn't sure if it was the humidity from the hot Houston night air or my nerves working overtime, but I was sweating like I'd been dancing in a Nelly video.

I bit my lip and looked around my bedroom. I was sitting on the window sill, trying to decide whether I should climb back in and take my butt to bed like I was supposed to or do what my heart was telling me to do and go meet my man.

I looked at the picture of my boo on my nightstand and knew that it was a no-brainer. Love wins every time.

We'd taken that picture six months ago in one of those dollar booths at the mall. It was so cute and we both looked so happy. That was the last day we'd been together before Keith had gotten arrested.

But he was out now, and was begging me to come meet him.

Did I mention how cute he was?

I know my mother would not understand anything about me leaving the house at two in the morning. If she woke up, I'd just have to deal with it.

My baby is worth it.

I eased over the sill and lowered myself down, almost landing in the bushes right outside my bedroom window. I paused, brushing the leaves off my Baby Phat jeans and pink shirt before taking off down the street.

I was trying to sprint to Keith's car but my strappy sandals slowed me down. It would be just my luck that a neighbor noticed me running down the street. Lord knows I wished they'd be entrepreneurs and get their own business so they could stay out of mine.

I made it to the entrance to my neighborhood in less than five minutes. A big smile crossed my face when I spotted my boo standing at the corner, leaning against a blue Monte Carlo.

"I can't believe it's you," I said as I threw my arms around his neck.

"In the flesh, baby. I was beginning to think you weren't going to come." Keith smiled back at me, looking cuter than ever with his big Afro, signature Sean John jeans and big white T-shirt. His golden brown skin was smooth and his body seemed even more in shape than I remembered.

"I'm sorry, but you know I had to sneak out of the house." I tried my best to sound sweet, but I think my voice sounded like I'd been sucking helium or something. I took a deep breath, trying to calm myself down.

"Yeah, I'm sorry about that, but I just got out and I called you as soon as I did. You look good, girl." He fingered one of my shoulder-length, jet-black spiral curls. I was glad I had made sure my hair was in place and my makeup was just right. I smiled at his compliment.

"Whoa." Keith leaned back and stared at me. "I knew something was different. You got your braces off."

I used to hate those stupid braces, but I was grateful now that my father had insisted that I get them. Not a day passed without someone telling me how pretty my smile was.

"You like?" I asked.

"Mm-hmm, but how could I have missed that? You know those things used to cut my lips all up," Keith joked.

I playfully hit him in the shoulder. He laughed as we climbed in the car and took off.

"So, why didn't you call me ahead of time, when you found out you were getting out?" I asked as we made our way onto the freeway.

"Man, I just found out. It was a big surprise. But I'm here now, baby. And with you, so that's all that matters." Keith looked over at me, squeezed my hand and smiled. "Girl, I missed you so much," he said.

I couldn't help but blush. Me and Keith had only been together four months before he went to jail, but I was madly in love with him and had no doubt he felt the same.

"So what happened? They caught the real carjackers?" I asked as I put my feet up on the dash.

"Baby, let's not talk about all that." Keith looked at my feet like they were the cutest things he'd ever seen. He shook himself out of the trance watching me seemed to be putting him in. "That place wasn't no joke. And I'm just happy to be out. You know I'm not a criminal." He took a deep breath, then stroked my cheek. "I missed you," he said again.

"I missed you, too." I leaned over and kissed him on the

cheek. "Hey, whose car is this, anyway?" I asked as I pulled myself away.

"My cousin Jerome's. I told him I had to come see my baby and he let me use it." Keith flashed another smile. "Did you bring the key?"

I reached in my jeans pocket and pulled out a single key. "Got it right here." I grinned. If my mother didn't kill me for sneaking out, she sure 'nuff was going to wring my neck if she ever found out what I was about to do.

"Cool, just tell me exactly how to get there. I know you said it's in Third Ward."

I dropped the key back in my pocket and leaned back in the seat and gave him the directions to my grandmother's house.

"Don't worry about a thing," Keith said. His calm voice eased my fears and I closed my eyes.

"You're going to go down to the third stop sign," I said once we'd reached our exit. "It's the first house on the right after the stop sign."

"Are you sure no one is going to come to your grandma's house?" Keith asked as we made the turn.

"I told you, I'm sure. My grandmother is in a nursing home and no one is ever at her house. I come by twice a week after school to water her plants, check on the cat and make sure everything is okay."

"Why don't y'all just sell it if your grandmother isn't coming back to it?"

"My mom was raised in this house and she'd never even think about selling it." And she would die if she knew I had

4

a boy up in there. *Stop thinking about your mother,* I snapped to myself.

I turned my attention back to Keith as he flashed that lopsided smile that had captured my heart. "Well, I'm glad you didn't sell it, because it's the perfect place for us to spend some time together," he said as he played with my hair.

I giggled and squeezed his hand.

"I also know if I'm with you I won't have to deal with Peanut and 'nem. You know they're worried that I might snitch on them," Keith said.

The smile left my face at the mention of Peanut's name. Keith was a good guy when I met him a year ago. Six months after we met he told me he didn't want to be just friends anymore, he wanted to be my boyfriend.

At the time, Keith was a straight A and B student. Then, right after we got together, he started hanging around his no-good cousin, Peanut. Then all of a sudden Keith started doing things he didn't have no business doing, like skipping school and riding around in stolen cars.

I'd cried like crazy when Keith got arrested. My mom didn't want me talking to him anymore, so I had to sneak down to the jail to visit him. I wasn't sure what to think about the whole situation, but when Keith told me that wasn't him on the Wal-Mart surveillance tape carjacking a little old lady, I believed him. After all, despite what my mother said, it wasn't like he was some thug or something. We both went to a nice high school. We both got decent grades and he had never been in any real trouble. Keith tried to play the bad boy to be more like Peanut, but never in a million years would he resort to carjacking.

However, that's just what the police said he did. That

seventy-eight-year-old lady had to be in the hospital for three weeks. The police caught Keith shortly after she was hospitalized. Someone had called Crime Stoppers and tipped them off.

"Right here." I pointed toward a huge yellow house on the right.

"Wow, that's tight," Keith said as he pulled the car into the driveway.

All that had happened three days ago. Since then I'd been coming by my grandmother's place after school every day. I'd even skipped school today, even though this was just the second week of school, and came straight here so we could spend all day together. It was days like today that I was thankful I had my own car. That way I could leave school with no problem and get home before my mother suspected a thing.

I'd surprised Keith by waking him up to the smell of frying bacon. I'd made a big breakfast, and even though I dropped shells in the scrambled eggs, Keith ate it like it was the best thing in the world.

We'd spent the day watching movies and just hanging out. After a long nap, I braided his hair while he played a PlayStation game his cousin had brought him.

"Baby, I like it." Keith rubbed his hand over his head as he checked out his hairstyle in the mirror. "I didn't know you could braid like this."

I smiled. Truth be told, I didn't like the braided hairstyle on him. But since he wanted that style . . . "Just one of my many talents," I joked.

"I don't know what I would do without you," Keith said, flashing a cute dimple at me. "Tell you what. I know you're tired of being stuck up in this house. Let's roll out. I need to go by Sharpstown and pick up a couple of outfits. Then maybe we can grab something to eat or something."

I looked at my watch. It was after three and school was just about to get out, so nobody would ask questions about me being in the mall. But that meant I'd have to find another lie to tell my mother. Oh well, I'll just say I had tutorials after school or something. "That sounds like a good idea."

"Let me hit the bathroom, grab my shoes and we can head out," Keith said as he leaned in and kissed me on the forehead. I loved the way his lips felt against my skin.

I watched Keith walk off toward the bathroom. If you had told me a week ago I'd be as happy as I was at this very moment, I would've told you you were on some serious drugs.

I knew I was being all giddy and stuff, so I tried to shake it off. I looked around for my grandmother's cat because I knew it was time for the mangy thing to eat.

"Garfield, where are you?" I looked throughout the house before knocking on the bathroom door. "Hey, Keith, you seen Garfield?"

"Yeah, the cat kept rubbing against the front door like it wanted to go out, so I let it out," Keith called out from the bathroom.

I exhaled in frustration and stomped toward the front door. There was no telling where that stupid cat had gone. The last thing I wanted to be doing was running through the neighborhood looking for Garfield.

I swung the front door open. "Garfield!"

"Freeze! Don't move!"

Three policeman stood on my grandmother's front porch with their guns pointed at my head.

To say I almost had a heart attack would have been an understatement. I almost peed in my pants. And in these sixty-dollar Apple Bottoms, that wouldn't have been a pretty sight.

"Put your hands in the air so we can see them!" one of the policemen shouted.

"What's going on?" I slowly raised my hands. I was so scared I couldn't keep my arms from shaking.

"Are you Camille Harris?" the cop to my right shouted.

"Ummm, yes. B-but what did I do?" I looked around at the cops.

No one replied. Instead, one cop motioned for another officer to go inside the house.

"Is there anyone inside?" the officer asked as he passed me.

"J-just my boyfriend."

In front of the house, more cops and the neighbors stared at me. My mother was going to kill me for sure.

"He took off!" The officer who had gone inside the house came back out yelling, "The bathroom window is open and he's gone."

The cop to my left yelled, "Spread out. He couldn't have gotten far." Into his walkie-talkie he said, "I want all patrols covering the area. Suspect fled on foot. He is in the area. Consider him armed and dangerous."

I shook my head. This had to be a bad dream. Armed and dangerous? What were they talking about? Who were they talking about? "Sir, could you please tell me what's going on?" I still had my hands in the air and my arms were starting to get tired.

"Who owns this house?" the officer asked.

"It's my grandmother's house," I nervously responded. "But my mother is the one who takes care of it."

"Does your mother know you're here?"

I shook my head. She didn't know but judging from the look on the officer's face, it was just a matter of time before she found out.

"What's her name and phone number?" The officer took out a pen and piece of paper.

"Lydia Harris. 713-433-7020." Tears rolled down my cheeks as he wrote down the name and number. "Sir, can you please tell me what's happening?"

The officer ignored my question, took my arms, pulled them down and placed them behind my back. "Camille Harris, you have the right to remain silent . . ." I tuned out on the rest of his speech when he snapped handcuffs on my wrists.

I was in full-fledged crying mode now as he walked me down the porch steps. "This must be some mistake. I didn't do anything!" I tried to tell him.

The officer finished reading me my rights as he placed me in the back of the patrol car.

"Please, officer. I didn't do anything."

"Didn't do anything?" The officer laughed. "Your boyfriend tried to choke a deputy before he broke out of jail last week. And you've been hiding him in your grandmother's house ever since. Harboring a fugitive is a pretty big crime." He slammed the car door.

Now, I was pretty sure he'd spoken plain English to me, but that mess he was talking sounded like a foreign language. Broke out of jail? Harboring a fugitive? In my grandmother's house?

But then I started thinking back over the last couple of days. How Keith didn't want to leave the house. How he was adamant that I didn't tell anyone he was there.

Oh. My. God. Maybe they would give me life in prison. Or the death penalty. Anything would be better than having to go home and face my mother.

2

Camille

She is about to get on my last nerve. I tried to tell myself
that my mother had every right to be going off like she was,
but honestly, I wished a Mack truck would come along and
plow her down. I don't want her dead or anything 'cause
she's still my mother. But maybe just laid up in a hospital
for a couple of days—anything to shut her up.

"And I've been telling you over and over, but do you listen? Noooooooo," my mother ranted. "You wanna act like
you're grown . . ."

Honestly, I wasn't listening right now, either. I was sick
and tired of hearing her go on and on. Yeah, I knew it was
wrong to let Keith hide at my grandmother's house. But I
didn't know he'd escaped from jail. Besides, he was innocent in the first place, which was probably why he'd broken
out. Why couldn't she understand that?

"It's those little fast-tail girls you hang around with.
That's what it is," my mother continued. "Got you thinking it's cool to be messing around with thugs."

I knew it was just a matter of time before she brought
up Melanie and Tonya, my girls from school. My mother
didn't like the way they dressed and said they were boy
crazy. Both of their mothers pretty much let them do what-

ever they wanted. I think that's what my mom didn't like most.

I looked over at my mother, who was still going on and on about how much I'd messed up. We were leaving the Harris County Juvenile Center, where we'd spent the last two hours signing all kinds of paperwork and pledging to the judge that I would remain trouble-free.

The last three days had been a nightmare. I'd been locked up in juvenile detention with car thieves, gang members and even a girl who had killed somebody. I probably slept eight hours the whole time I was there. Those girls were mean, and twice somebody tried to pick a fight with me. I'd read enough books about people on lockdown to know what goes down in jail—I knew I had to act hard to keep people up off of me. It also didn't hurt that one of the detention guards had taken a liking to me and kind of watched my back. Even still, it was an experience I would never forget. I couldn't wait to get home and write in my journal about my whole experience. With all the drama with my mama, my journal is the only thing that keeps me sane.

But right about now, listening to my mom rant, I was starting to wonder if I'd have been better off behind bars. Especially when I noticed the tears streaming down my mother's face—again.

"I just don't know where I went wrong with you." She wiped her tears, then pounded the steering wheel. "I tried, Lord knows I tried. I work to give you the best of everything and this is how you repay me? You get arrested. For hiding a fugitive. Your daddy is probably turning over in his grave . . ."

There goes the daddy card. That really made me feel

bad. Nothing's gone right since my dad died last year. I hoped my father wasn't looking down on me, as my mother always claimed he was.

". . . then you just sit over there and act like you don't care. I just don't understand you, Camille." She shook her head in exasperation. "Since you've been in the pen, they caught your little car-thieving boyfriend," my mother snapped, letting her anger overtake her tears.

I let out a long sigh. "I wasn't in the pen, Mama."

"The pen, juvie, it's all the same. My point is that little thug is back behind bars."

"He's not a thug, Mama."

"He is a thug, just like the one who took your daddy's life. I can't believe you're still defending him! Jesus, be my guide," she moaned. I knew that was coming, too. The seventeen-year-old boy that shot my father had a long police record.

"Do you think that boy has given you a second thought?" she continued. "He just took off and left you high and dry."

"He just didn't want to go back to jail, that's all."

"He shoulda thought about that before he stole that car from that poor little ol' lady and dang near killed her."

"He said he didn't do it."

"And I say I can sing like Diana Ross, but I can't."

"He needed to be out to prove his innocence." I didn't know why I was still defending him. There was nothing on earth I could possibly say to convince my mother to lighten up on Keith. Shoot, I'd been trying myself to make sense of why Keith had broken out of jail and gotten me caught up in all of this madness.

My mother let out a crazy laugh. "You've been watching

too many movies, girl. Besides, he's on videotape. You know where the news said they found him?"

I shrugged as I looked out the window to see where we were. I was anxious to get out of the car and away from my mother.

"He was with his girlfriend."

I snapped my head toward my mother. "What?"

"Oh, did that get your attention? You want to talk to me now?"

"What are you talking about?"

"I'm talking about they found that little nappy-headed boy at his baby mama's house," she said as she wagged her finger at me.

I glared at my mother. "You're just saying that to hurt me."

My mother reached behind her seat, pulled up a newspaper and tossed it at me. "Don't take my word for it. Read it yourself."

I grabbed the paper and immediately began reading the story underneath a mug shot of Keith. " 'Wanted fugitive Keith Lee, seventeen, was captured Friday at his girlfriend's home in Wharton, Texas,' " I read out loud. "Police say Lee's nineteen-year-old girlfriend, who is also the mother of his one-year-old son, had been hiding him for the last week. Authorities had closed in on Lee, who was in custody for a carjacking, as he hid in the home of a relative of a friend last week. Lee escaped then, but the friend, Camille Simone Harris, sixteen, was taken into custody and charged with harboring a fugitive.' "

My heart dropped through my stomach.

"Umm-hmmm, you go to jail for that fool and you're just a *friend*. Did you know you were just a *friend*? Seems to me like you thought you were his girlfriend. Humph.

Threw your life away for a *friend*. Got your name all up in the paper for a *friend*." My mother shook her head. "How am I supposed to show my face around church? My child's name all up in the paper. That boy just played you like your name was Monopoly. You ruined your future for him and he was just playing you all the time. . . ."

I tuned out my mother's rants. I was too busy fighting back the tears that had already begun trickling down my cheeks. I'd risked everything for Keith and he had a girl-friend. And a child! How could I be so stupid?

My tears must have gotten to my mother because she softened her tone. "Baby, I'm sorry. I don't mean to make this any worse for you. I'm just very angry and disap-pointed."

I balled the newspaper up and stared out the window as the tears continued to flow down my face.

"But you know, baby," my mother continued, "the Lord says out of the darkness shall come light." She pulled the car in front of the huge church. "And we should just count our lucky stars the judge didn't send you to jail and is let-ting you take part in this community service group. What's it called again?"

I sniffed. "Good Girlz."

"Good Girlz. I like that. That's what you need in your life right now, to surround yourself with good girls. Hope-fully they'll be a positive influence on you."

I stared out the window as my mother pulled into a parking spot. "But this is a church."

"This is where they meet. And, this is where you need to be."

Not only was I *not* looking forward to spending my time meeting up in some stupid community service group,

I definitely wasn't interested in sitting up in some church bonding with a bunch of Goody Two-shoes. But right about now, my choices looked slim. Juvie or the Good Girlz. Or even worse, stay at home every evening and listen to my mother tell me how wrong I'd been about Keith. Nope, out of the three, I would definitely be bonding with the Goody Two-shoes.

3

Camille

I *so* do not want to go in there.

My mother jumped out of the car and ran inside the church. But me, I was in no hurry to get inside Zion Hill Missionary Baptist Church. I leaned back in my seat. Two hours a night, two nights a week inside some church spilling all my business to a bunch of strangers. That was my punishment. The judge had been adamant that the Good Girlz program would help me "refocus." I'd thought the program was at a community service building or something, not a church. That must've been what the judge had been whispering to my mother about during their meeting. I should have known something was up, the way my mother's mood changed after talking with the judge.

I finally opened the car door and followed my mother inside. She was probably already in the church office, no doubt begging the receptionist to save her wayward child.

I took my time heading inside. I looked around the parking lot. Multicolored windows adorned the large red-brick building, and a white cross sat on the front lawn, towering above the church. I was just about to go inside when I noticed a pretty Hispanic-looking girl with long black hair leaning against the side of the building. She was wearing a cheap-looking black warm-up suit and her eyes were puffy and red, like she'd been crying for days. She held a duffel bag in front of her and a piece of paper clutched in her hand.

"Hey, are you okay?" I asked.

The girl nodded, and a tear rolled down her cheeks. *Great.* It seemed rude to leave her outside crying, so I asked, "Are you sure?"

The girl nodded again.

"What, you don't know how to talk?"

The girl stared at me like she was sizing me up. "I'm sorry. I'm just . . . I don't know . . ."

I looked through the glass door and saw my mother had taken a seat.

"You can't be no worse off than me," I sighed as I turned my attention back to the girl. "I'm Camille."

"I'm Angel."

I glanced at the duffel bag. "Are you going somewhere?"

Angel bit her lip as she pulled the bag closer to her.

I debated whether I should try and figure out what was wrong with her. Shoot, I had enough to deal with myself. Besides, I knew I should be getting inside before my mother started trippin'. "So, what are you doing standing out here by yourself?"

Angel shrugged. "I don't know. I just saw this and came here." She handed me a piece of paper, which I read. It was a flyer about the Good Girlz' first meeting at the church tonight.

"Oh, yeah. That's what I'm here for."

Angel pointed to the bottom of the flyer. "It said they were doing a raffle for twenty-five dollars. I . . . I could really use that."

I looked at Angel like she was crazy. Why would someone want to come to this meeting on their own, even for twenty-five dollars?

Angel must've known what I was thinking. "I . . . I'm getting ready to move and I need to try and get some money."

"And you think twenty-five dollars is gon' help you move?" I looked at the duffel bag again. "Are you a runaway?"

Angel sighed like she didn't want to answer a bunch of questions. "No, I just want— Look, you think they'll let me come to this meeting?"

I shrugged. "I don't know. This is my first time here. I'm just coming because I didn't have a choice."

"Oh."

By this point, my mother had appeared in the doorway. "Camille, what are you waiting on? Miss Washington, the church secretary, is waiting to meet you," she called out. "Don't think you're getting out of this."

Since my back was to her, I rolled my eyes. Where was that Mack truck? "Well, I gotta go. It was nice to meet you," I told Angel.

"You, too." She looked pitiful as I started to walk away.

I took a couple of steps then turned back to her. "Are you just gon' stand out here?"

Angel seemed unsure of what she should do.

"You know what, why don't you come inside with me? This is supposed to be a church, they can't turn you away. I'm sure that's in the Bible or something," I said.

Angel looked hesitant. "How long you think this will last? I need to be outta there before it gets dark and really, I'm just hoping I can win that money."

I shook my head. This girl sure was hard up for twenty-five dollars. "Like I said, I have no idea. But you ain't gon' know if you don't go in," I said.

I guess she decided I knew what I was talking about because she followed me in. Of course, the church secretary welcomed us both. After we got situated, my mother waved good-bye, grinning at me like this was summer camp or something.

"I'm going to run some errands and I'll be back in two hours," she said.

I watched her leave. "Finally, some peace and quiet," I muttered.

"What did you say?" Angel asked.

"Nothing," I said, looking at the clock on the wall. "We still have thirty minutes before the meeting starts. You want to run across the street to the store with me to get a soda?"

Angel nodded and for the first time since I had met her, she smiled.

4

Camille

Angel ducked behind me like she'd known me all her life. We were standing outside the convenience store across the street from the church. And it was obvious some stuff was about to go down.

"Yo' mama so fat she got her own zip code."

We watched the boy walk in circles around a tall, heavy-set girl. Even though she towered over him, he looked like he was having fun teasing her.

"You got one more time to talk about my mama," the girl growled.

"Or what, Jasmine? You'll eat me?" The boy busted out laughing and his four friends joined in.

"Yo' mama's hair so short she roll it with rice." The boy cackled.

"Dedrick, I'm 'bout to show you something funny, all right." Jasmine balled up her fists.

"Yo' mama . . ."

Jasmine didn't give him time to finish his mama joke. She lunged at him and knocked him to the ground. She jumped on his stomach and began pounding him in the face.

"Aaaaghhh!" Dedrick screamed as he kicked wildly. "Get this big Amazon off of me!"

The more he called her names, the more Jasmine kept hitting him.

"Should we do something?" Angel whispered to me. We'd stopped right outside the door to the convenience store when we saw the small crowd gathered.

"Are you crazy? That girl don't need no help," I replied. I was not about to get caught up in a fight, even if it was an unfair one. But judging from the way Jasmine was beating that boy, there was nothing unfair about it.

"Help me! Somebody call the cops!" Dedrick screamed. None of his friends moved. They all looked stunned, maybe too scared that Jasmine's blows would catch one of them.

I was the only one who noticed the woman walking out of the store. Her reddish-brown hair was pulled up in a French roll on top of her head. She had on a long skirt and hooded long-sleeved shirt.

"Oh, my God. Jasmine?" she said as she rushed over and tried to pull Jasmine off of Dedrick. "What are you doing?"

Jasmine snatched her arm away from the woman. "I'm about to kill him."

The woman, who looked like she was in her late twenties, stepped in front of Jasmine. "Would you calm down?" she said.

"Miss Rachel, I'm gon' hurt him," Jasmine said, her chest heaving up and down.

"It looks to me like you've already done that." She turned to Dedrick. "Are you going to be all right?"

"If you keep Bigfoot away from me," he said as he struggled to get up off the ground. His lip was bleeding and there was a bruise forming underneath his eye. He was definitely no longer laughing.

"I got somewhere to put this big foot," Jasmine said as she lifted her leg like she was about to kick him.

"Jasmine!" Rachel snapped. "Look," she said, turning toward Dedrick and his friends. "You boys get on out of here. Go home before you get in any more trouble."

A couple of them looked like they wanted to say something, but the mean mug on Jasmine's face stopped them in their tracks. They helped Dedrick up, then walked off mumbling.

"Now, do you want to tell me what you, a young lady, are doing outside the neighborhood corner store fighting a boy?" Rachel said.

"Miss Rachel, I don't mean no disrespect 'cause I know you used to babysit me growing up, but I don't need no babysitting anymore. And I will fight Dedrick or any other boy that steps to me the wrong way."

"So fighting is your solution to everything?" Rachel asked.

"No, but I'm sick of people treating me like dirt. It ain't happening no more. I ain't gon' let it happen no more."

Jasmine finally noticed us staring at her. "What the heck y'all looking at?"

I just stared at her. Angel scurried into the store, saying, "I'm going to use the restroom."

I picked up the pay phone and acted like I was using it.

Jasmine rolled her eyes and turned back to Rachel. She looked like she was fighting back tears. "I can't help my size, Miss Rachel."

I pretended to talk on the phone while I sized Jasmine up. I could see why people were teasing her. Homegirl had to be at least six feet tall, two hundred and forty pounds.

She didn't look sloppy fat or anything, just big. The Nike jogging suit and LeBron James sneakers she had on definitely weren't doing her any justice. She was actually pretty cute, with a baby face that made her look like she couldn't be a day over fifteen. She had thick honey brown hair, which she wore pulled back in a ponytail.

"You know what you need?" Rachel asked.

"What? To leave this stupid place?" It looked like she was trying to keep from crying.

"And go where?" Rachel replied. "No, you need to come with me this evening."

"With you where?"

"I'm on my way to a meeting. It's a new community service group at the church we've started. It's called the Good Girlz."

My ears perked up when she said that and I leaned in trying to listen to their conversation. They were headed to the same place I was.

"Yeah, right. Like I'm a good girl." Jasmine snorted.

"It's not like that at all," Rachel responded. "It's a group for girls who strive for the goodness in their lives, who want good things."

"Who doesn't want good things? It's actually getting them that's the hard part," Jasmine replied.

"Well, that's the kind of stuff we'll be talking about. That, self-esteem and a whole bunch of other fun stuff, all while being a service to the community."

"Oooh, what fun," Jasmine replied sarcastically.

My thoughts exactly.

"Actually, it *will* be a lot of fun," Rachel shot back. Jasmine still looked like she couldn't care less. "We're giving away door prizes tonight, including cash money. I know you could use a couple of extra dollars in your pocket."

"How much you giving away?" Jasmine finally seemed interested.

"You'll just have to come to the meeting to find out." Rachel smiled. "Come on, Jasmine. You'll like it. We're going to take trips and do lots of fun stuff. I'm really excited about it. It's going to be a small group and I know everyone will love it."

"Miss Rachel, not to be funny, but you don't strike me as one who should be leading a group of girls. I heard all about your past and your drama." Jasmine's scowl finally turned into a half smile.

"No, on the contrary, Jasmine, my past makes me an excellent person to lead this group." She grabbed Jasmine by the hand. "Come on. I'm on my way now; don't worry, there won't be anyone there to pick on you."

Jasmine tried to pull her arm back. "I just wanna go home."

Rachel turned to her, a stern look on her face. "The more I think about it, the more I think you need this group. Now, you come with me, or I will call your grandmother and tell her that you've been fighting again."

Jasmine looked like she was thinking about it. "Fine, but don't look for me to get all saved and sanctified 'cause I'm going up in a church."

Rachel laughed. "Okay. I promise I won't make you get saved and sanctified if you promise to stop jumping fourteen-year-old boys in parking lots."

Jasmine laughed. "Dedrick is fifteen."

"Whatever," Rachel replied. "Just no more fighting, okay?"

Jasmine nodded. "No more fighting."

Rachel smiled and motioned for Jasmine to follow her. I waited until they walked off, then hung up the phone. Good grief. What had I gotten into? A runaway, a supersize fighter and an instructor with a whole bunch of drama of her own. Boy, this group was going to be loads of fun.

5

Camille

$\mathcal{I}$ stood outside the small meeting room and checked out the girls inside. There were four other girls there besides me and Angel. One of them, a high yellow girl with a Beyoncé weave, was busy primping in the mirror. Then there was the weird-looking chick dressed in all black sitting in the corner. She looked like a serial killer.

Another girl was looking around nervously like she was scared to death that someone was about to steal her lunch money. Maybe she was scared of Jasmine, who sat two seats down from her. Jasmine's scowl was back and she looked like she would hit anybody who even looked at her the wrong way. She sat in a chair with her arms crossed and her legs gaped wide open like a guy. She looked like she really didn't want to be here.

"I know that feeling," I muttered.

"Did you say something?" Angel whispered. She was the only person who seemed halfway interested in being there.

I shook my head. "Nah, just ready to get this over with. Come on."

I walked into the room with Angel close on my heels. "What's up, y'all?" I was trying to be friendly to these losers as I sat down next to the scary girl.

Angel gave a meek wave and sat down next to me.

Jasmine didn't reply. Neither did Goth girl. Scary girl looked away and Miss Prissy kept flinging her hair.

"I guess these stuck-up girls are too good to speak," I told Angel loud enough for them to hear.

Jasmine sat up in her seat and dropped her arms like she was ready to rumble. "Who you calling stuck-up when you all up in other people's business?"

Now, I know I had just witnessed this girl beat the crap out of a guy, but for some reason I wasn't intimidated. Don't get me wrong, I'm definitely not a fighter, but I'm no punk, either. "If the shoe fits."

Jasmine stood up and started walking toward me. I kept my game face on but I couldn't help but think if she hit me, I was gon' have to grab something and try and knock her out because no way could I win a fistfight with her.

"Now, I know you two are not about to fight up here in the Lord's house."

We all turned toward Rachel, who had just stepped into the meeting room. No one answered her.

"Jasmine, you promised no fighting," Rachel said as she walked into the room. "I go into my office for one minute and walk back out here to find you all at each other's throats before you even know one another's names." Rachel walked to the front of the room and sat her Bible and a folder down on the podium. "Rule number one: There will be absolutely no fighting in this church."

"Then you better tell this pint-size freak to leave me alone," Jasmine said as she glared at me.

I had my nerve back now that Rachel was in the room to keep me from getting killed. "I guess everybody would be pint-size to you, you—"

"Enough!" Rachel snapped.

"You better tell her, Miss Rachel," Jasmine said.

"I got this, Jasmine. Sit down." Rachel turned toward me. "You have a seat, too." She waited for both of us to sit back down. "Now, this is not the way I wanted us to get things started. We are in this for the long run, so we might as well all learn to get along." Rachel took a deep breath, then flashed a bright smile. "Let's start by introducing ourselves. I'll go first. Welcome to the first meeting of the Good Girlz. For those of you who don't know, I'm Rachel Adams. I'm the First Lady of Zion Hill and the founder of the Good Girlz. Don't let the name fool you. We're not trying to make you out to be Goody Two-shoes."

I tried not to smile. She must've been reading my mind.

Rachel continued. "But we do want to get you to realize that you are entitled to the good things in life. None of us here are better than anyone else. We all have issues and our goal is to help each other work through them. We'll also take part in some service activities and do our share of giving back to the community."

Rachel clapped her hands together. She was obviously excited about this program. "We will deal with your issues and discuss ways we can live more godly lives."

I couldn't help but let out a disgusted sigh. Here we go with the preaching.

"But first, let's start by just having everyone give their names. Then we'll come back and let you tell a little about yourself," Rachel continued.

Angel introduced herself first. Then me, then everybody else. The scary-looking girl was Sasha. Tameka was the girl dressed all in black like she was going to a funeral or something. And the diva over there was Alexis.

"Now, let's move on and talk about ourselves." Rachel smiled at us, but I wasn't taking the bait. "When I say we all have issues, I just want you to know that includes me. While I'm a proud First Lady now, and the daughter of a preacher, I ain't always been holy." She stopped and laughed, piquing my interest.

"Even now, it takes a lot of effort for me to walk the straight and narrow. I'm a preacher's kid . . . and you know what they say about preacher's kids."

"Y'all the worst ones," I offered. The other girls laughed along with me. Except for Jasmine. She still had a scowl.

"I don't know about all preachers' kids, but I can tell you this preacher's kid was pretty bad," Rachel said. "Any crazy thing you've done behind a boy, I've already done it. Any disappointment you might have given your parents, been there, done that. So I'm hoping you all will get to the point where you will feel comfortable opening up." Rachel turned toward me. "Your turn. What's your name?"

"Camille Harris."

"Okay, Camille Harris. Where are you from and what made you come here?"

The smile left my face. I didn't want to sit up in church and lie but I still wasn't feeling letting these girls all up in my business. "I'm from the southwest part of Houston. I go to Madison High School and I'm here, umm, because my mom thought it would be good for me."

Rachel looked at me like she knew there was more to the story. "Okay, I'm sure we'll get more in depth later."

I was grateful that she didn't push it and instead moved on to the scary-looking girl.

"And you would be?" Rachel asked.

The girl didn't respond.

"You don't have to be nervous," Rachel said.

She still didn't say anything.

"How about we come back to you?" The girl nodded and Rachel gave her a reassuring smile.

"Tameka, why don't you come out of the corner and come up here and introduce herself."

Goth girl looked like she wanted to crawl up in a hole and die. She reluctantly moved toward the front of the room.

"My name is Tameka. I go to Hightower High School," she all but whispered.

"Tameka is my niece," Rachel said proudly. "She lives in Missouri City, but she's here because I'm trying to expose her to different things, right?"

Tameka groaned, but didn't say anything.

"She's a little shy," Rachel said. "But we're going to work on that in this group. Right, Tameka?"

Tameka shrugged. Rachel sighed before turning her attention to Angel. "Your turn," Rachel said.

"Hi, I'm Angel. I attend Westbury High School, at least for now, anyway. I don't know if I'm going to stay there, because . . . things aren't going too good for me right now."

Rachel pressed on. "And why aren't things going well?"

Angel sighed. "I, um, I had to move away from my neighborhood."

"Where are your parents?" Alexis asked. I didn't even know she knew how to talk in complete sentences, since she hadn't bothered to say anything more than her name.

Angel looked real uncomfortable. "Me and my mom, well, it's just me." Angel puckered her lips together like she wanted to say more but she kept quiet.

"Oh, snap. I bet she's a runaway," Jasmine said.

"I am not a runaway," Angel protested. She shot Jasmine a mean look. "I'm staying with my sister right now."

"Whatever." Jasmine shrugged. "I just think you need to stop lying, that's all, especially all up in a church."

Angel glared at Jasmine like she couldn't stand her. "My mom didn't want me there. Does that make you feel better?" she snapped.

For once, Jasmine looked apologetic. "Dang, I'm sorry."

"I came here because stuff is tight with my sister and . . ." Angel dropped her hands in her lap and turned toward Rachel. "I was just hoping to win the drawing you were gon' have tonight because I really need the money." She looked like she was trying not to cry.

Rachel walked over to Angel and took her hands as she sat down next to her. "Angel, God doesn't do anything by chance. You are here tonight for a reason. He put that flyer in your hand. He led you here because He knew you need what this group can offer."

I tried not to turn up my nose. What could this group possibly offer besides wasting my time? *Stop with all the negativity,* this little voice in my head seemed to say. I turned my attention back to Rachel.

"Whatever demons you are wrestling with, we want to help you work them out." Rachel squeezed Angel's hand before standing up and walking back to the front of the room. "Part of our problem in trying to live a Godly life is that we don't know we're being attacked. Drugs, alcohol, whatever drives you away from a Godly life is a tool that the Devil uses to attack you."

I really was not trying to hear a sermon. I was tired and ready to get home. Rachel must've read the look on my face because she said, "And the Devil also messes with our mind

so that we can't receive the Word when it's being fed to us."
She smiled at me and I immediately felt embarrassed.

"Amen to that."

We all turned toward my mother, who stood in the meeting room doorway. She was wearing a gigantic smile.

"Can you tell them that again?" my mother said.

I couldn't help but groan as my mother walked into the room. She stuck her hand out toward Rachel. "I'm Mrs. Harris, Camille's mother."

Rachel shook her hand. "Nice to meet you."

"Sorry to interrupt, but Mrs. Washington said you'd be finished by seven," my mother said.

Rachel looked down at her watch. "Wow, I can't believe time has flown by that quickly." She looked at all of us. "We will wrap up for today but think on these two things. I want us to create a bond here and that means you all will communicate outside of the group. I want everyone to make sure your numbers are correct on this paper." Rachel handed a piece of paper to me. I reluctantly took it.

"I'll make copies for everyone and have them at the next meeting. I also need to give away that door prize I advertised," Rachel said.

Angel perked up.

"Normally, I would do a drawing," Rachel said. "But I want our first lesson of our group to be one of selflessness. How about we all agree to give it to Angel?"

Angel smiled as she nervously looked around.

"Anybody have a problem with that?" Rachel asked.

Me, Alexis, and Tameka shook our heads. Jasmine shrugged.

Before I knew it, I found myself saying, "I think that sounds like a good idea."

"Then it's a done deal." Rachel reached into her Bible and pulled out an envelope. She handed it to Angel. "I know you said you came for the money, but I hope you'll come back because you like being with us."

Angel blushed. "I will."

Rachel dismissed the group and we all headed for the door. Just a few minutes ago I was itching to get out of here, but as I looked at my mom standing in the doorway with that big stupid grin, I realized my two hours there weren't so bad after all.

6

Camille

I knew I could no longer avoid a conversation with my mother.

I'd managed to escape a bunch of questions yesterday when my mother picked me up from the meeting by pretending I really had to get some studying done. Yeah, I was lying again, but I wasn't in the mood to get chastised about Keith and answer a hundred and one questions about what happened at the Good Girlz meeting. So now we were in the car, on the way to the senior citizen center to visit my grandmother. And I was trapped—no escape.

"I think that group is just going to be wonderful for you." My mother beamed as we drove along Highway 59.

I sighed. "You would." My mother loved anything even remotely related to church. We practically lived in church. It's not that I minded going, just not every single night. Sundays were enough. I mean, really, God knows I'm busy so I'm sure He doesn't expect any more than that.

"Yes, that's just what you need in your life right now," my mother continued. "I mean, just look at how you all gave that young lady that money with no protest."

"Mama, it was twenty-five dollars."

"Still, just the look on everyone's face, like you wanted

the girl to have it. That was God at work in that room."
My mother wagged her finger. I tried not to roll my eyes.
What was the big deal?

"Yep, this group is definitely going to help you turn
your life around," my mother said as the sounds of Mahalia
Jackson blared from the car stereo.

"My life doesn't need turning around, Mama," I replied
as I reached up and turned the radio from KTSU 90.9, my
mother's favorite gospel station, to my favorite hip-hop station, KBXX 97.9. I pepped up when I heard Kanye West's
song, "Golddigger." I turned up the volume and started
bobbing my head.

My mother slammed the off button on the radio. "Have
you lost your mind? Turning off Mahalia for that mess?
That's what's wrong with you young women today. That
fool up there talking 'bout golddigging women and you
think that's some type of compliment."

I leaned back in the seat and exhaled in frustration. I'll
be so glad when I'm grown. "Mama, it's just a song."

"A song that got you thinking it's cute to be a golddigger."

Parents are a trip. It's a stupid song. That's it.

"You need to be listening to gospel music, that's what
you need. Not this foolishness Kanye is singing about," my
mother said.

"I will have you know, Mother, that one of Kanye West's
biggest songs is 'Jesus Walks,' " I said defensively. She was
talking about my future husband and I wasn't having that.
Kanye is one of my favorite singers, which of course was
just another reason my mother wouldn't like him.

"Jesus walks where?" my mother said.

"That's just the name of the rap song, Mama."

"Oh, Lord. Now they rapping about Jesus. What is this world coming to?" My mother shook her head in disgust.

I turned my attention out the window. I don't even know why I bother trying to debate anything with my mother anyway.

I was grateful my mother turned her attention back to the radio and was now humming along with some old-sounding person, singing about a river in Jericho.

We pulled into the senior center, parked and made our way inside. I hated this stale-smelling place but I loved coming to visit my grandmother.

"Guess who?" I said as I eased open the door to my grandmother's room.

My grandmother was sitting in her rocking chair by the window, knitting, something she loved doing. She was wearing her usual white housecoat and matching slippers. Her gray hair hung loosely on her shoulders. Her wrinkled skin gave away her age—seventy-nine—but her eyes were vibrant and young. She always said it was because she was happy about life and while her body got old, her spirit did not. She didn't get around much because she had arthritis really bad, which is why she was living in the senior center. My grandmother looked up and smiled.

"Well, since Oprah just left I don't guess it would be her," she said as I walked into the room. "Oh, it's Princess Diana!"

I laughed and raced over and hugged her. "Oh, you got jokes, Granny."

My grandmother kissed me on the cheek, then hugged Mama, who'd come in behind me.

I sat down on the floor next to my grandmother. I loved being around her and hated seeing her stuck up in this place. We'd tried to get her to come live with us, but she said she liked her independence in the assisted living center. Besides, she said she didn't want to leave her friends.

"To what do I owe this pleasure of a visit on a weekday?" my grandmother asked.

"We just came by to see you since we didn't make it last Sunday," my mother said as she sat down on the bed.

"Yeah, Granny, we missed our visit since you kicked us to the curb for the bingo tournament," I laughed.

"Baby, that was the bingo championship. You know I'm the bingo queen." Grandma held up an arm to show her muscle. I laughed at the sight of her skin hanging from her arm.

"Mama, you know you don't need to be gambling," my mother chastised.

My grandmother rolled her eyes. "Bingo ain't gambling." She leaned in to me. "Why your mama got a stick up her butt?"

"Mama!"

"What?" She smiled and winked at me. I was trying my best not to crack up. My grandmother always did know how to make me laugh.

"Well, we'll see if you're laughing when I tell you what your granddaughter did," my mother said with a serious look across her face.

I immediately stopped smiling. I couldn't believe my mother was about to open her big mouth.

"I wasn't gonna tell you because I didn't want to worry you, but I think you should know." She stopped and shot me a disappointed look. "Your only granddaughter snuck a boy in your house. And not just any boy. A fugitive. A thug. A carjacking, escaped convict."

My grandmother's eyes grew wide. "What you say?"

"Then, when the cops showed up, the little punk took off and left Camille to take the rap. She got arrested and everything." My mother crossed her arms. "So your granddaughter is now officially a statistic—a hard-core criminal."

At that very moment I couldn't stand my mother. I lowered my head in shame because I hated my grandmother knowing anything bad about me. Imagine my surprise when my grandmother started laughing!

"So you been in the joint? Spent time with the po-po?" She cackled.

I tried not to smile. "Granny, you've been watching too many Madea movies."

My mother was obviously frustrated. "This is not a laughing matter. This is serious. She could've ruined her life."

"Calm down, Lydia," my grandmother said. "And tell me what happened."

"We went to court and the judge said if Camille takes part in this church youth group it won't go on her record."

My grandmother nodded. "Then she'll participate in the youth group, right, baby?" she said as she reached out and took my hand.

"That's right, Grandma."

"There." My grandmother patted my hand, then turned to my mother. "No need to get your panties all in a bunch. We make mistakes and we learn from them."

"But, Mama, this is serious. She could've gotten in serious trouble. She's just lucky—"

"I seem to recall a certain someone calling herself running off with a no-good Bobby Byers when she was sixteen and he left her stranded in a whole other town."

"Mother!" My mom jumped to her feet. I looked at my grandmother in shock.

Grandma smiled and nodded her head. "I'm just saying, everybody makes mistakes. God doesn't condemn us forever, so we shouldn't condemn one another. I'm sure she knows what she did was wrong and it won't happen again." My grandmother looked at me for reassurance.

"It won't," I promised.

My mother sighed in frustration and plopped back down on the bed. I smiled up at my grandmother. "You're the best, Granny."

"So are you, baby." She lifted my chin. "And don't let anyone—especially some little boy—treat you like you're not."

I nodded and spent the next few minutes enjoying the silence as my grandmother softly stroked my hair. And I have to admit, I couldn't help but take pleasure in watching my mom fume because my grandmother had taken my side.

7

Camille

The clock seemed to be going backward. How was I ever going to make it through six months of these meetings? We'd only been at tonight's meeting for twenty minutes and while Rachel was funny, I just wasn't feeling this Dr. Phil/Oprah warm and fuzzy counseling.

Rachel had been going on and on about how important it was for us to learn to love ourselves. I definitely didn't need to hear all of that because I already loved myself—I just loved Keith, too. But for some reason my grandmother's words kept playing in my head. *Don't let anyone treat you like you're not the best.* Keith didn't actually treat me bad, I kept telling myself. He was just scared. That's why he took off. I can understand that.

I suddenly realized I hadn't been paying attention to anything Rachel was saying. I scanned the room. Angel was the only one who looked enthusiastic about being here. Jasmine wore an expression that said she definitely wasn't looking to make friends. She looked like a loner who took pride in being a loner.

Miss Thang, a.k.a. Alexis, was acting like she couldn't care less about anybody's situation. I might have to agree with Jasmine about her because if anybody was acting like a snob, that girl sure was. She was dressed in a short denim miniskirt and a tank top that had the word *Diva* across the chest. She was wearing a Louis Vuitton belt to match her backpack purse, which she hadn't even bothered to take off.

Rachel turned to Beyoncé and asked her to tell us more about herself.

"My name is Alexis Lansing. I live in River Oaks and attend St. Pius private school. My father owns the Lansing Hotel, the only minority-owned hotel in the country," Alexis responded with her nose in the air.

I let out a long huff. Who asked her about her dang daddy and who cares what he owns?

"I am here because I am a member of the Junior League and part of our community service requires that we donate our time to needy causes," Alexis continued.

I caught Jasmine's eye and we both looked at each other like we wanted to throw up. Jasmine fought back a laugh as I put my finger in my mouth like I wanted to gag.

Rachel shot me a chastising look and I straightened up. Alexis, however, didn't notice—or didn't care.

"My daddy says you should always help those less fortunate and you don't always have to do that through money, although we have plenty of that. But you can do it through time or sharing of your talents. I'm here to share my talents."

"Give me a break," Jasmine mumbled.

Rachel ignored Jasmine and smiled at Alexis. "Well, Alexis, we are happy to have you here sharing your talents." She turned toward the scary-looking girl. "Sasha, tell us why you've joined the group."

The girl didn't say anything. She just sat there with a nervous look on her face.

"Do you know how to talk?" Jasmine chimed in.

The girl twitched and shot her head around toward Jasmine, who slowed her words and started acting like she was doing sign language. "Why are you here?"

We all snickered. Scary girl started shaking. Jasmine slowly leaned in toward her and yelled, "Boo!"

Scary girl nearly knocked over her seat as she took off running. Her sudden exit caught everyone, even Jasmine, by surprise.

Rachel shot Jasmine a mean look before taking off after the girl.

"Maybe she had a nervous condition," Alexis said after Rachel left the room. "My daddy knew this lady who stayed in her house all the time because people made her nervous."

"Don't nobody care about your daddy," Jasmine snapped.

Alexis looked shocked. Jasmine got up and pranced around the room with her hands on her hips. "My daddy is rich. My daddy owns all of the United States and Canada. My daddy bought me this hoochie mama outfit. My daddy makes me think I'm all that, when I really ain't nothing."

Alexis frowned and narrowed her eyes. "At least I know my daddy. Your ghetto behind probably don't even know who your daddy is."

Angel's mouth dropped open. I tried not to laugh. Who knew Alexis had spunk like that? Jasmine, on the other hand, didn't think anything was funny. "No, you didn't."

Alexis stood up to face Jasmine. It didn't seem to faze her that she was almost a foot shorter than Jasmine. "Yes. I did."

Jasmine took a step toward Alexis.

"Jasmine! Sit your tail down!" No one had noticed Rachel come back in the room. "This is ridiculous. We are supposed to be here getting to know each other, not fighting like cats and dogs."

"You need to get that pit bull under control," Alexis said, pointing to Jasmine. "Because she's confused if she's letting the prettiness fool her. I will stoop down to her ghetto level and beat her like she stole something."

Everyone seemed a little shocked because even though she was still talking all proper, Alexis's snotty air had disappeared and the street had come out in her.

"Nobody's going to be doing any beating around here," Rachel said. "Both of you take your seats. Jasmine, I hope you're happy. Sasha isn't coming back. You scared her off."

Jasmine shrugged like she couldn't care less.

Rachel sighed in exasperation. "Jasmine, have you ever thought about why people pick on you? Maybe it's because you're a bully yourself."

Jasmine folded her arms, but refused to answer.

Rachel shook her head before turning back to the group. "Okay, we're starting over. You're next," she told Jasmine.

Jasmine rolled her eyes but still didn't respond.

"Tell us about yourself or I'm calling your grandma and telling her about you fighting and that other little secret we share," Rachel threatened.

"Fine. I'm Jasmine."

"And what school do you go to?"

"Madison."

A surprised look crossed my face. Madison wasn't so big that I wouldn't have recognized someone like Jasmine.

"I haven't seen you around," I said.

"Maybe because I don't want to be seen," Jasmine replied.

"Jasmine lives in the Third Ward and she just transferred to Madison a couple of days ago, right?" Rachel asked.

"That ain't her business," Jasmine replied.

Rachel let out a long breath. "Do you want to tell the girls a little about yourself?"

"Not really."

"Jasmine!" Rachel snapped.

"Fine. I'm the second to the oldest of six kids. I'm always broke. I don't know my father. And, oh yeah, I hate people. Anything else you want to know?"

Rachel inhaled like she was trying not to go off on Jasmine. "Okay, Jasmine, tell the group why you are here."

" 'Cause you made me come."

Rachel covered her eyes in frustration. "Jasmine, we will come back to you." She turned to Alexis. "Let's get back to you, Alexis. I know you said people seem to think your life is perfect." Rachel hesitated and smiled. "But surely there must be an issue that weighs heavily on your mind sometimes?"

Alexis finally lost that air of confidence and lowered her eyes. She looked like she was debating opening up. "I don't have a whole lot of friends," she said softly.

"Surprise, surprise," Jasmine remarked.

"Jasmine!" Rachel snapped. "I'm not going to tell you again."

"Sorry," Jasmine mumbled.

Rachel turned back toward Alexis. "Why do you think you don't have a lot of friends?"

I could tell Jasmine wanted to say something smart.

"You know, maybe it's something I really shouldn't be talking about," Alexis said as she looked nervously around the room.

"Or maybe you do need to talk about it. Talking through our issues helps us work them out," Rachel said. "One of the things I want us to be clear about in this group is that we all have faults. None of us should ever sit in judgment of another. The only judge in your life should be God."

Alexis looked like she was weighing Rachel's words. She hesitated before saying, "Okay. Don't ask me why I'm telling you guys this, but it's something I've never told anyone else."

8

Alexis's story

One year earlier

"I just don't understand it. You said this place would help her," my mother said as we sat in the doctor's office discussing my sister, Sharon. "She doesn't appear to have made any progress."

"Well, as I've been telling you, some of our patients just develop slower than others," Dr. Molina replied. I liked the handsome, curly-haired doctor. He seemed like he was genuinely concerned about my sister. Too bad my mother didn't think so.

"You've been saying that 'develop slower' mess for the last six years, but this is getting ridiculous," she said. "Sharon turned nineteen yesterday and she still functions like she's six years old."

I sat next to her in the plush doctor's office at Memorial Greens Psychiatric Hospital. I hated coming to this place because it made me want to cry. Some of the people here were scary and most of them were crazy. Sharon wasn't crazy, just developmentally challenged, as my mother called her.

"She is making progress, Mrs. Lansing," Dr. Molina said. "She's become really good friends with another patient named Jada and they spend a lot of time together. That's a positive sign."

My mother crossed her legs and narrowed her eyes. "Not to be disrespectful, Dr. Molina, but I'm tired of signs. I need results."

"Mrs. Lansing, as I told you when you brought Sharon to us ten years ago, she may never progress. Mental retardation has varying degrees."

"Don't call my baby retarded!" mom snapped.

"That's not what I was saying," Dr. Molina protested. I knew the doctor was getting tired of my mother. Every month it was the same thing. She'd come here demanding results. She'd always get the same answer, yet she still was always going off. I figured it was because she was used to getting her way with everything and everybody and she didn't know how to handle *not* getting the results she wanted.

"Mama, can I go see Sharon?" I asked. I wanted to get out the room and visit with my sister a little while before it was time to go.

"That's fine. Just don't go any farther than Sharon's room," she said before turning back and going off on the doctor some more.

I sighed as I made my way down the long hall. My mother had tried to care for Sharon at home, but when she almost burned the house down by playing with matches in the middle of the night, we'd moved her here with the hope that the hospital—one of the best in the country—would help her get better. So far, it wasn't working.

I peeked into Sharon's room. She was there with another pretty young girl and an older-looking woman.

"Hi," I said as I entered the room.

"Alexis!" Sharon said, bouncing off her bed and racing to hug me. I smiled at her. She was absolutely beautiful, with long curly hair, bright eyes and the cutest dimples I'd ever seen.

"Where's Mommy?" Sharon asked.

"She'll be here in a minute," I said. "What are you doing?"

Sharon took my hand and dragged me over to the girl. "This is my friend, Jada," Sharon said excitedly. I forced a smile even though it hurt me to see my sister act like a little girl.

"Hi," I said to Jada. The pretty chocolate-colored girl with the empty look on her face smiled back but didn't say anything.

"She's a little shy," said the woman who was standing next to her. She stuck out her hand. "I'm Aja, Jada's sister."

I shook her hand. "Nice to meet you."

"Jada's my best friend in the whole world," Sharon said as she wrapped her arm through Jada's.

Aja looked at both of them and smiled. "It seems our sisters have taken a liking to each other." Aja reached out for Jada's hand. "Jada insisted I come down and meet Sharon. But Jada, it's time for us to go. Let's let Alexis spend time with her sister."

"Nooooooo!" both of them wailed together.

I couldn't take the sight of my sister crying. "No, it's fine. She can stay. I just wanted to say hi."

"Hi," Sharon said, calming down some. "See you later."

I smiled. "Mama will be in here to see you in a minute, okay?"

"Okay."

I waved good-bye to my sister and went to wait in the

hall for my mother. Five minutes later she appeared, ducked in Sharon's room and must've gotten the same reception because five minutes after that, she was walking out.

"Let's go," my mother said as she hurried out of the room.

I jumped up and followed her, knowing not to say anything until she was ready to talk. While I liked visiting my sister, I hated what it did to my mother afterward. She would spend the next few days locked in her room, not talking, just sleeping and being in a foul mood. According to my father, Mama was severely depressed. She blamed herself for Sharon's condition even though the doctor said it was nobody's fault that Sharon was born with a rare gene that made her that way.

With my father always off on business and my mother constantly in a world of her own, I didn't know what to do to make my family better.

"So you have a sister with special needs?" Rachel said after Alexis finished with her story.

"Yes." Alexis lowered her head.

"And? What's the big deal about that?" Jasmine asked.

Alexis cut her eyes at Jasmine. "You wouldn't understand." She turned back toward Rachel. "My family has this image that they try really hard to maintain. My mother is a former president of Jack & Jill, and she gets invited to all the society functions. Her uppity friends would have a heart attack if they knew she had a daughter like Sharon."

"So you mean nobody knows?" I asked.

"Nope, except for a few relatives. My mom would die if

she knew I told you all. I really think she means well. She just thinks if people know about Sharon they'll start to feel sorry for her and stuff. And she can't stand people feeling sorry for her."

"Wow," I said. "You have a sister you can't talk about. That's messed up."

Alexis shrugged. "I'm used to it by now."

We all sat in silence for a few minutes. Even Jasmine seemed at a loss for words. Rachel finally spoke.

"Well, we may not always understand our parents' motives, but it's important to respect their places in our lives," she said.

All four of us looked at Rachel like she was crazy. Rachel laughed. "You don't see it yet, but you will. Trust me, I should know."

I shook my head. She obviously didn't know my mother. "Whatever. My mom is coo-coo for Cocoa Puffs, so I don't see that happening. Ever."

"You can say that again," Jasmine laughed.

Rachel smiled as if she had something up her sleeve.

9

Camille

I hate school. With a passion, I hate it. Don't get me wrong, I'm good at it. I just can think of a hundred and one things I could be doing with my time rather than sitting up in a bunch of boring classes, learning a bunch of things I probably will never use again.

I grabbed my Economics folder and closed the door on my locker. I checked out my watch and saw that I had less than one minute to get to my next class. The last thing I wanted was Mrs. Reed breathing down my neck about being late again, so I raced down the hall to her classroom.

Mrs. Reed was just another reason I didn't like school. She was my demanding Economics teacher and refused to let me skate through like I did in all my other classes. My mother was always claiming that one day I would thank Mrs. Reed for pushing me so hard. Yeah, right. I wouldn't hold my breath.

"You just made it, Miss Harris," Mrs. Reed said as I slipped in the door just as the bell rang.

"I had to—"

"Please, no excuses, Miss Harris. Just take your seat and open your book to chapter eleven." She turned back toward the class. "We were talking about the laws of supply and demand . . ."

I took my seat in the back row and tuned out Mrs. Reed. I didn't understand how one person could get so excited about economics.

I spent the next fifty minutes fighting off sleep and watching the clock. When the bell rang, I was one of the first ones out of my seat and headed for the door.

"Miss Harris, please remain behind," Mrs. Reed called out.

I groaned and took a seat at a desk in the front row and waited for the last student to leave the room. Mrs. Reed closed the door and walked over to the desk. *What did I do now?*

"Miss Harris, you do not apply yourself the way I believe you should. However, the fact remains that you are excellent at economics. I have a new transfer into one of my classes, and I was hoping you would help her catch up with where we are, as well as share some of your notes in preparation for next Friday's test."

I stared at Mrs. Reed like she'd lost her mind. "You're kidding me, right? I don't have time to tutor anyone."

"Now, Miss Harris, you know me well enough to know I don't kid. And I didn't say anything about you tutoring anyone. All I need you to do is help her get up to speed."

Before I could protest, Mrs. Reed walked toward the door. "This student is new here and is very quiet. I'm hoping you can not only help her with economics but help her get settled in here." She opened the door and waved for someone to come inside.

I nearly fell out of my seat when Jasmine walked in with her usual mean look plastered across her face. Her backpack was slung loosely over her shoulder. She had on an Adidas warm-up suit and her hair, as usual, was pulled back in a ponytail. Maybe if she didn't dress and act like a boy, people would stop treating her like she was one.

"What's up?" Jasmine said as she slid into the desk next to me.

"Nothing. What's up with you?" I shot back.

"Oh, so you two know each other?" Mrs. Reed asked.

"Kinda sorta," I said.

"Good, that will make this relationship even better." Mrs. Reed began straightening papers on her desk. "Now, Camille, you have computer lab right after this, correct?"

I nodded.

"Well," Mrs. Reed continued. "I've taken the liberty of talking to your lab teacher and she has agreed to let you spend this period helping Jasmine get ready for the big test on Friday."

I wanted to protest, but I knew Mrs. Reed. Protesting would only make things harder on me in the long run. Besides, Jasmine didn't seem like she wanted to be here any more than I did.

Mrs. Reed walked toward the door. "I'm going to the teachers' lounge for a bit. You two can continue to use my room."

Mrs. Reed left, and Jasmine and I sat in silence.

"So, you need some help with economics?" I finally said when it became obvious Jasmine wasn't going to say anything.

"I don't need no help with anything," Jasmine said.

"You need help with English," I mumbled.

Jasmine sat up in her seat. "What did you say?"

"Dang, nothing. Chill out," I flashed a smile, hoping to tame the beast. "Why are you always so worked up?"

Jasmine grabbed her backpack and slammed it down on the desk. "Because I'm sick of people giving me a hard time." She unzipped her backpack and pulled out her economics book. "Let's just get this over with."

I stared at Jasmine. Although she wore a mean look, her eyes looked so sad.

"Can I ask you a question?"

"Can I stop you?" Jasmine said as she flipped open her book.

"Why'd you transfer here?"

Jasmine paused like she was contemplating whether she wanted to open up to me. She sighed. "Fighting."

Somehow that didn't surprise me. "Oh."

Jasmine looked at me like she was waiting for me to start talking about her. "You heard me when I said I was sick of being picked on. Kids at my old school were always giving me a hard time. One day, I'd had enough and kicked this girl's tail. So they kicked me out. I finished last year at an alternative school, then transferred here this year. You got a problem with that?"

"Hey, I have no problems. Besides, I understand," I said. "The only thing is, these kids around here aren't much better."

Jasmine exhaled in exasperation. "Can we just do this? I hate economics as it is. Now I've transferred to this dumb school and I'm behind. No way will I be ready for this test."

I laughed. "With Mrs. Reed, none of us ever are."

Jasmine seemed to relax. "Is she hard?"

"As hard as they come." I looked around, then leaned in and whispered, "But one of my friend's sisters had her years ago and she says if it wasn't for Mrs. Reed working her so hard, she didn't think she'd have made it to college."

"Why are you whispering?" Jasmine asked.

"I don't know. I guess I don't want Mrs. Reed to hear me giving her props. Knowing her, she's got this place bugged."

Jasmine laughed. "So, I guess she was right when she said all of our hard work here will pay off."

"That's what they say." I leaned back and returned to my normal tone. "Personally, I'll have to see it to believe it."

We began going over the stuff that would be covered on the test, then reviewed my notes for about thirty minutes. When the bell rang, I began gathering my stuff. "I think you've got this."

"Thanks for the help, Camille. Where are you headed from here?"

I was shocked at Jasmine's niceness. "Algebra. What about you?"

Jasmine looked at her schedule, which was taped to the front of her notebook. "I have Spanish with Mr. Wright."

"Oh, that's down the hall from where I'm going. I'll wait on you." I was surprised that Jasmine and I clicked because Jasmine definitely wasn't the type of girl I would hang around under normal circumstances.

Jasmine had just zipped her backpack when the door swung open and a cute, short brown-skinned guy came waltzing in.

"What's up, Camille, hid any fugitives lately?" he said.

I rolled my eyes. "What's up, C.J., stole anybody's candy money lately?" I asked, referencing a rumor going around school that C.J. had stolen candy money from the school fund-raiser.

"I didn't steal no money and you need to quit saying that." C.J. turned his gaze toward Jasmine. "And who might this big, fine thang be?"

I groaned. "Please, boy. This is my friend, Jasmine." Jasmine seemed shocked that I'd called her a friend, but I didn't linger on it. "She's new and she doesn't want your little Tiny Tim behind."

"It ain't the boat in the water, it's the motion in the ocean," C.J. said as he licked his lips and walked closer to Jasmine.

Jasmine stuck out her hand to keep him from coming any closer. He barely reached her neck. "Fool, please," Jasmine said. I couldn't help but notice she said it with a smile, though.

"C.J., you are so corny. Come on, Jasmine." I grabbed Jasmine's arm and pulled her toward the door.

"Don't listen to her, Jasmine," C.J. called out. "She's just mad because she wanted me and I wouldn't give her the time of day. But you, baby, you can have all the time you want. I could—"

I let the door slam on C.J.'s words. "That is exactly why I don't mess with guys around here," I said as we walked down the hall.

I looked over at Jasmine and stopped when I saw the starry-eyed expression on Jasmine's face. "I know you don't like him!"

Jasmine snapped out of her daze. "Huh? Girl, please. That buster?"

I stared at Jasmine, trying to gauge if she was telling the truth.

"I know the pickings are slim around here, but C.J. is not the answer. Besides, his sister Tilly is crazy and very overprotective of any girls trying to talk to her brother," I said as Jasmine started walking again.

I shook my head when Jasmine didn't respond. Yeah,

Jasmine was hard-core, but underneath that tough exterior she was starting to seem soft. We stopped in front of Jasmine's Spanish class.

"This is Mr. Wright's class," I said.

"A'ight. See you later." Jasmine waved and walked inside. Her eyes had gone back to that wispy look.

"I need to work fast and get her looking like a girl before she thinks all she can get is boys like C.J.," I muttered as I watched Jasmine sit down with her legs gaped open.

10

Angel

"The meeting of the Good Girlz Club will now come to order." Rachel stood at the front of the meeting room. Everybody was here again, with the exception of Sasha and Tameka.

Once again I was the only one interested in being there. I don't know why the others bothered coming, since they acted like they hated it so much. But me, I'd been in such a funk lately that I was willing to try anything. I had nowhere else to turn, so I had to at least give this place a try. I wasn't going to let these grumpy girls ruin tonight's meeting. Maybe Rachel would even give out some more money. My fingers were crossed.

"How is everyone?" Rachel asked.

"I'm fine, Miss Rachel," I responded. No one else said anything.

Alexis was picking at her nails. Jasmine had her usual snarl on her face. Camille was fidgeting in her seat.

"Where's Tameka?" I asked, trying to break the silence.

"Tameka won't be coming anymore. Let me just say my niece is a work in progress. I will try to get her to rejoin, but for now it will just be us," Rachel responded. She walked to the front of the room, pulled up a chair and sat down. "Let's go ahead and start today's session by talking about our biggest issue. Alexis, since you shared with us the other day, why don't we start with you?"

Alexis looked up like she just realized she was in the room. "Huh?"

"I said, what's your biggest issue?" Rachel repeated.

Alexis looked confused.

"Probably what color to paint her nails." Jasmine smirked.

Alexis turned around in her seat and glared at Jasmine, who was sitting several seats back. "What is your problem with me?"

"Don't you two start," Rachel said.

"No, we just need to settle this right here and now. I want to know, what is your problem with me?" Alexis focused all of her attention on Jasmine.

Jasmine leaned forward. "You want to know what my problem is with you? I can't stand how you sit over there thinking you better than somebody. You think 'cause you rich that everybody is beneath you. You turn your nose up at everybody like your stuff don't stink. Yo' bougie self ain't all that."

Alexis looked like she was fighting back tears. That surprised me because Alexis had already proven that she could hold her own against Jasmine. "I already told you my world ain't perfect. Besides, you don't know anything about me," Alexis said.

"I know what I see and I don't like what I see."

"You know what?" Alexis swung her long hair as she turned back toward the front. "You don't have to like me. Besides, I wouldn't expect you to anyway because it's obvious you don't even like yourself."

Rachel must've decided it was time to jump in. "Okay, I see the first issue we need to deal with is each other. First of all, Jasmine, how can you draw a conclusion about Alexis when you don't even know her?"

Jasmine leaned back, crossed her arms across her chest and cocked her head. "I can look at her and tell I don't like her."

"That's what's wrong with so many teenagers today. You look at someone and they look different from you—they're a different race, they wear their hair differently, they talk differently—and you assume you don't like them, when in actuality, you don't know anything about them," Rachel said.

"Yeah," Alexis chimed in. "Nothing at all."

Rachel turned to her. "And Alexis, oftentimes people do think they're better than someone else just because they have more money in the bank or they go to what is perceived to be a better school. Just because life has been better to you, the truth is you're no better than anyone else."

Alexis leaned back in her chair but didn't say a word.

"I guess you told them, Miss Rachel." Camille threw in her two cents.

"Well, Camille, since you and Angel have been so quiet this evening, why don't you start by telling me what your biggest issue is."

Camille laughed as she crossed her legs. "That would be my mother, no doubt."

Rachel joined her in laughter. "I remember I used to think the same thing when I was your age." She turned back to the group. "How many of you would say your relationship with your mother or father is your biggest issue?"

All four girls slowly raised their hands.

"Angel, let's start with you. Why do you have a problem with your mother?" Rachel asked.

There wasn't enough time in the world for me to go there. "You don't even wanna know."

"Yes. We do," Rachel replied.

I took a deep breath. I hadn't shared my secret with anyone. I didn't even know these girls like that, so why should I open up to them? I don't know how Alexis let people all up in her business. That's not me. Rachel must've been reading my mind.

"Angel, I know we've all just met, but I can feel it already: We have a bond. And by opening up to each other, we'll only make that bond stronger."

I thought about what she was saying. I did come here because I was at the end of my rope and didn't know what to do. "Where do I begin?"

"How about at the beginning," Rachel said.

"You might want to take a seat, Miss Rachel, 'cause my story might take a minute."

11

Angel

Six months earlier

"*Oye mamá pequeña, usted es uno perro bonito.*"

I couldn't take my eyes off the drop-dead gorgeous guy with the green eyes who had just told me that I was one pretty dog.

"Excuse me?" I said.

He kept his smooth demeanor as he stepped a little closer, leaned to my ear and repeated his sentence. "*Oye mamá pequeña, usted es uno perro bonito.*"

I couldn't help but burst out laughing at him.

We were standing in the food court of Sharpstown Mall, where I had spent the afternoon shopping with my sister, Rosario. The food court was packed and I was waiting in line to get a pretzel. I knew I looked good in my candy-apple red tank top and black lowrider jeans.

He looked like he could be Usher's twin with his baby soft, light brown skin and smooth fade. He wore an Allen Iverson jersey and baggy jeans.

"You want to tell me what's so funny?" he asked.

"Do you know what you just said to me?" I had stopped laughing, but was still giggling like crazy.

He suddenly looked unsure of himself. "Yeah, I said, 'Hey little mama, you are one pretty lady.' "

"No," I said, trying not to laugh since it was obvious he didn't find anything funny. "You said I am one pretty dog."

"What?"

"*Perro* means dog. Where did you learn your Spanish?" I said with a smile.

He suddenly cut his eyes at a group of guys standing nearby. They were cracking up laughing.

He then turned back to me. "I'm sorry. My boys have a warped sense of humor. One of them speaks Spanish and he told me to come tell you that when I told him I wanted to holla at you."

I blushed. Although guys told me how pretty I was all the time, I had never really given them the time of day. I figured, why bother? My mother had made it clear that I couldn't date until I turned eighteen anyway.

But there was something about this guy. He brought butterflies to my stomach. And the way he looked at me made me feel like someone special.

"Let's start again," he said, sticking his hand out. "Hi, I'm Marcus, and you are one pretty lady."

I smiled. "Hi, Marcus. I'm Angel." I shook his hand.

"That name fits you well because you remind me of an angel," he replied as he let my hand go. We talked for the next thirty minutes, until Rosario came and got me in the food court. I'd taken his number, since there was no way I could give him mine. I called him that night after my mother went to sleep. We talked for almost an hour each night for the next three nights straight. I finally agreed to meet him at the mall again and we'd just started hanging out from there.

I couldn't believe my luck. Not only was he good-looking, but I loved his personality. He made me laugh constantly and we spent every moment I could get away from school and my mother together for the next two weeks. Then one day while we were hanging out at his house, he said he was ready to take our relationship to the next level.

I spoke out in protest. "Marcus, I told you, I really want to save myself for marriage."

"Come on, now," he pleaded. "You been listening to that nonsense your mama spouting. Nobody waits these days. Besides, my brother told me the Bible said if two people are in love, it's fine."

I racked my brain, but in all my years of Bible study, I didn't ever remember hearing or reading that. "You're making stuff up, Marcus."

"No, I'm not," he responded. "They just don't teach it because they don't want us to know that."

I shook my head. I wished he would stop pressuring me. Staying true to my word was hard enough as it was. On my thirteenth birthday, my mother had made me promise not to lose my virginity until my wedding night. My friends said that was the dumbest thing they'd ever heard, but so far, I'd kept that promise. It had cost me a few interested boys, but I'd taken pride in the fact that I was saving myself for marriage. But that was before Marcus. I'd never felt about anyone else the way I felt about Marcus.

"Come on, Angel. You know I love you." Marcus got

up and paced back and forth across the cluttered living room. He'd convinced me to skip school and meet him at his house, a decision I was now starting to regret.

"You know I'm seventeen. A man. You can't really expect me to wait to be with you," he turned to me and said matter-of-factly.

I felt my heart drop. The thought of Marcus with someone else tore at my insides. He must have sensed it because he said, "If you won't do it, you know somebody else will." He reached down, pulled me up off the sofa and moved in close. He then lifted my chin and looked into my eyes. "And that would really make me sad, because all I want is you."

I swear I wanted to pass out right there. As much as my head said no, I found myself following my heart. The next thing I knew I gave in to Marcus. It was quick and painful, and it wasn't even all that. It must not have been for him either because he didn't call for two weeks afterward.

When I finally reached him by phone, he gave me some excuse about his grandmother being sick. He promised to call, yet days later, he still hadn't. He broke my heart. But that was nothing compared to how I felt two weeks later when I found out I was pregnant.

I was in tears as I told Rosario, the only person I could talk to. Rosario had been disowned herself after getting pregnant, even though she was twenty-one when she had her baby. Our mother said she had shamed the family because she was having a baby without a husband. Rosario had told me that whatever I did, don't tell our mother I was pregnant.

But I knew who I had to tell—Marcus. I thought maybe if Marcus agreed to marry me, my mother would take the news a lot better.

After a few days of casing out his house with no luck,

I finally managed to track him down as he was leaving the campus with some of his friends.

"What's up?" he said when he saw me walking toward him.

"Hi," I said softly. I wanted to be mad but I was so nervous I couldn't even concentrate. I was just hoping he wouldn't take the news too hard. "I've been trying to get in touch with you."

"Sorry, I haven't been around. You know how it is." Marcus's friends stopped and stood behind him.

I eyed them nervously. "Can I talk to you alone?"

"Why don't we go to my house and talk? My mom won't be home for another few hours." He grinned slyly as he placed his hands around my waist.

"Marcus, I can't."

He stepped back, agitated. "Here we go with this again. Angel, I told you, I don't have time for this." He turned to his friends. "Let's roll."

"Marcus, I'm pregnant," I blurted out as he walked off.

He turned and looked at me dumbfounded.

"Did you hear me?"

He slowly nodded, then seemed to come out of his daze. "So, what does that have to do with me?"

It was my turn to be dumbfounded. "You're kidding me, right?"

He stuck out his chest, acting hard in front of his friends. "Naw, I ain't kidding. Don't act like that baby is mine. I ain't fixin' ta be nobody's daddy."

I stared at him in disbelief. "What? Marcus, you know I've never been with anyone else!"

"I don't know nothing. Shoot, in fact, Lance told me he got with you."

I felt my eyes water. It was taking everything in me not to cry. I didn't even know who Lance was. "That's not true and you know it."

Marcus turned back toward his friends. "Lance, didn't you get with Angel here?"

Lance looked confused for a minute, then said, "Sure did. Tony, you did, too, huh?" motioning to another friend.

"Yep, and my boy over at Sterling said he did, too," Tony laughed.

I frantically looked at each of the boys. "Why are y'all lying on me?"

"The way I see it"—Marcus gave me a mean look I had never seen before—"anybody can be your baby's daddy. So don't go pinning that on me or I'll make sure everybody knows how you slept around. You get rid of it and we can go back to kickin' it. Otherwise, I suggest you lose my number." Marcus turned and signaled for his friends and they all walked off.

When I finished my story, every eye in the room was on me.

"You're pregnant?" Camille asked, an astonished look on her face.

I lowered my head in shame.

Alexis leaned in and peered at my stomach. "You don't look pregnant."

"Five months." I pushed my baggy T-shirt in. "The big clothes hide it."

"Wow," Camille said as she touched my stomach. "I do see a pudge."

Rachel had a sad look across her face. I could tell she was disappointed as well. "Does your mother know?"

I shook my head. "It would break her heart. She worked so hard to provide for me and give me a good life. I just couldn't bear the thought of her being so disappointed in me. I wasn't ready to face the look on her face when she found out. Plus, I wanted to leave before she kicked me out."

Rachel gently took my hands. "Sweetie, you have to tell her. You can't do this on your own. Besides, how do you know she would've put you out?"

I started crying softly. "I just . . . I don't know. I just can't tell her."

"There is no question about it. You have to tell her," Rachel said. "You can't run forever."

I could feel Jasmine's stare piercing my back. I knew Jasmine would have something to say. "What?" I sniffed. "Why are you staring at me like that? Say what you gotta say."

"See, that's why guys mess with dumb broads like you," Jasmine said as she took in my story.

"Jasmine," Rachel snapped, "I can't believe you! That is not nice."

Jasmine shook her head in disgust. "But it's true. She let that boy whisper in her ear, then knock her up."

"I don't—"

I held up my hand and cut Rachel off. I didn't even have the energy to argue with Jasmine. "Don't worry about it, Miss Rachel," I said. "Jasmine is right. I was dumb, real dumb. I thought he really loved me and I let him run game and talk me out of the thing that meant the most to me—my body. I haven't talked to Marcus since then. He changed his cell phone number. I never had his home phone number and every time I go over to his school, he loud-talks me and embarrasses me. But it's what I deserve."

"Forget that." Alexis finally jumped into the conversation. "You know you can get a DNA test when your baby gets here and make him pay child support."

"Yeah, right." I gently rubbed my stomach. "Marcus doesn't have a job and he made it clear that he wants nothing to do with me or my baby."

I looked away when I saw Rachel's eyes fill with tears. I couldn't take the look of pity on her face.

"That's the type of thing young women need to think about before deciding to get intimate with someone," Rachel said. "You should always ask yourself, 'What if?' Put aside everything about it being biblically wrong since I know you guys aren't even in that mind-set. But just ask yourself, 'What if, by some chance, I do get pregnant? Is this the person I would want to be my child's father? Will I be a good mother? Am I even ready to be a mother, period? Can I emotionally and financially support a child?'" She paused like she was trying to see if her words were sinking in.

"Not to be disrespectful, Miss Rachel, but that's a whole lot to be thinking in the heat of the moment." Camille seemed to be trying to lighten the mood.

Rachel smiled. "That's the whole problem. You let some little boy feed you lines and you get all hot and bothered and lose all good sense. And sometimes, you can pay for that one moment of judgment lapse for the rest of your life. Trust me, I speak from experience."

Jasmine got up, walked over to the refreshment table and picked up a chocolate chip cookie. "Well, you ain't gotta worry about that from me, 'cause I ain't gon' let some boy tell me anything and make me sleep with him," Jasmine proclaimed as she popped a whole cookie in her mouth.

"That's because you don't have to worry about some boy trying to sleep with you at all," Alexis mumbled.

"What did you say?" Jasmine started toward Alexis.

"Ladies, please," Rachel said. Both of them cut their eyes at each other before Jasmine sat back down in her seat. Rachel turned her attention back to me.

"So, Angel, if you could do it all over again, what would you do differently?"

"Stick to my guns," I said. "I would've waited, I guess. What am I supposed to tell my baby? Her daddy don't even like her? I just feel like I let everybody down."

"See, that's what I'm talking about," Jasmine said. "That's just dumb. Why wouldn't you use protection or something?"

If only she knew. I let out a crazy laugh. "That's the sad part. We did. You know how they teach us in health class that protection isn't foolproof?" I ran my hands over my stomach. "This is proof that they were telling the truth."

Jasmine, for once, appeared speechless.

Rachel stood up and placed her hands on my shoulders. "Angel is right, the only foolproof way to make sure you don't get pregnant is to not have sex," she said.

"So, you don't think your mom will forgive you?" Camille asked.

I bit down on my lip before speaking. "At first, I was thinking she would. But I know my mother. She can never forgive this. I mean, I wonder if God will even forgive me. My mother is always preaching about right from wrong and she says when I make a mistake, I have to be punished."

"Man, your mama sounds like she's in one of them cults or something," Jasmine remarked.

"I told you before, God doesn't punish us," Rachel said.

"So are you saying God approves of her being pregnant?" Camille asked.

"Of course not," Rachel responded. "He's disappointed, but that doesn't mean He's going to punish you for the rest of your life."

As much as I wanted to believe her, I just didn't believe it could possibly be that easy. All my life I'd heard how vengeful God was. If I broke a lamp, my mother threatened that God would "bring down His wrath" on me. If I was misbehaving in any way, my mother would warn me that "God was watching."

Alexis raised her hand. "I don't mean to cut you off, Miss Rachel, but it's after seven and my mother is texting me." She held up her cell phone. "She needs me to bring something home and she told me to hurry up."

Rachel looked at her watch. "Wow, time just flew by again today. I'll see you all Thursday. Same time, same place."

As the girls rose to leave, I lollygagged around. I wasn't looking forward to the long walk to my sister's house, especially at this time of night. Honestly, I didn't want to go to my sister's at all.

Rachel immediately noticed. "Angel, how about you come home with me? And Jasmine, don't you be late Thursday, because it'll be your turn to share your story." Rachel grabbed my hand and walked out before Jasmine could protest.

12

Angel

Okay, this pineapple upside-down cake tasted like it had been baked by Betty Crocker herself. I stuffed another piece into my mouth.

"Miss Rachel, this cake is off the chain," I said with my mouth full.

"Thank you, but chew your food before talking. I know your mother taught you better than that." Rachel winked.

"You know she would be having a fit right now," I replied after swallowing my food.

Rachel smiled as she sat down at the kitchen table across from me.

"I'm serious when I say you should really talk to your mother."

I put my fork down. "I know you're right. I just have to get the strength to do it."

"Well, I'll be praying for you," Rachel said. "And I want you to pray, too."

I wanted to tell Miss Rachel that really wasn't an option. It had been a long time since I prayed. And after what I'd done, I was sure God wasn't trying to hear anything I had to say.

Luckily, before I could respond, the kitchen door

creaked open. A tall, light-skinned man with reddish hair walked in, followed by two adorable children.

"Hey, honey," the man said as he leaned down and kissed Rachel on the cheek.

"Mommy!" the little girl said as she ran and threw her arms around Rachel's neck.

"Hey, my beautiful family." Rachel turned toward me. "This is my husband, Lester; my daughter, Nia; and my son, Jordan. Everyone, this is Angel, one of the girls from the group."

The girl smiled brightly but Jordan just grunted as he walked over to the refrigerator and opened the door. He looked like he couldn't be more than eleven or twelve. He had cute dimples and looked like a male version of Rachel.

"Jordan, don't be rude," Rachel said as he started moving stuff around in the refrigerator. "Get out of the refrigerator and say hello to our guest."

Jordan slammed the door shut and turned to me. "Wuz up?"

I smiled, even though he was acting just like a little brat. "Hi."

"Wuz up?" Rachel asked. "Boy, is that how you talk to someone?"

Jordan didn't respond. "Can I go to my room now?" he asked.

Rachel huffed, then waved him off. "What is his problem?" she asked Lester.

"What is always his problem? Mad at the world," Lester replied as he loosened his tie. "You know he didn't want to go to vacation bible school in the first place. He sat up there pouting all night."

Lester reached his arms out to Nia, who jumped up and

clung to him. "I'll go give the kids their baths. Nice to meet you, Angel," he said.

"You, too, Mr. Adams." I watched them walk out of the kitchen. They looked like such a happy and normal family. Why couldn't I have a life like that? My father is in prison and my mother is a religious freak.

"Are you okay?" Rachel asked.

"I'm fine. You have the perfect life." I knew I sounded jealous, but I just wished I could have been born into such a picture-perfect family.

Rachel laughed so loud it caught me off guard. "Child, please. My life is anything but perfect. I told you I was a teenage mom. Twice. And there was nothing pretty about my life. Things were hard for me. And I did a lot of stupid things."

"Yeah, but you turned out all right. You're with your children's father, you have this nice house and everything," I said as I looked around the kitchen of Rachel's massive five-bedroom home. The kitchen itself was bigger than my mother's living and dining rooms combined, and it was decorated like something out of a professional magazine.

"See, that's what's wrong with young people today," Rachel said. "You see my life and think, oh, she had a baby when she was a teenager and she's fine. But what you don't know is that I had more than my share of heartache to get to this point. I wish more young girls knew my story. They would see all that glitters ain't gold."

Rachel seemed lost in her own world for a minute. I almost hated to interrupt her, but I had been dying to ask her a question all evening. I finally decided to spit it out. "Miss Rachel, do you think I should give my baby up for adoption?"

Rachel snapped out of her daze and focused all of her attention back on me. "Sweetie, I can't answer that question. That's a question *you* need to answer. But you do need to respect your mother enough to sit down and talk to her about it."

I leaned back against the chair. I knew Miss Rachel was right, but my mother was a different type of woman. If you looked up *stubborn* in the dictionary, my mother's name, Christina Lopez, would be right next to it. I sighed. "I don't know how I'm going to take care of a baby. But I don't know that giving my baby away is the answer, either." I sat silent for a moment, wondering what I should do next.

"Where are you staying tonight?" Rachel finally asked.

I knew that was coming. "I guess I'm going over to my sister's house." I looked at my watch. "Shoot, she's already left for work. I was gon' have her come get me." I hated lying to Miss Rachel, since she was so nice to me, but I didn't want her to know I was walking over to my sister's.

"Then it's settled," Rachel said. "You'll spend the night here. In my guest room."

I didn't expect that. "I can't ask you to do that."

"You didn't." Rachel stood up. "Come on. I'll run you a nice, hot bath, let you relax, and then you can sit up and watch movies until you fall asleep. It's not like you have to get up for school tomorrow. It's a teacher conference day, isn't it?"

I nodded. I was glad for the break from school. Now that I was starting to show, I didn't know if I could deal with the stares and comments at school and all my teachers looking at me like they were disappointed in me.

"Good," Rachel replied. "So you can sleep in as long as you'd like."

I smiled as I stood up to follow Rachel. "Thank you so much."

"My pleasure."

Thirty minutes later, I was dressed in one of Rachel's T-shirts and nestled under the covers in Rachel's guest bed. It felt so good to be in a bed, especially a plush bed like this one. I definitely had to get myself a plan so I could stop sleeping on my sister's living room floor.

13

Camille

The smell of mothballs filled the room. Alexis covered her nose as we made our way over to a rectangular table in the cafeteria of the Julia C. Hester House for the Sick and Shut In.

I sat the big box of games down, then reached in and handed Alexis the bingo cards. "Here, pass these out."

Alexis looked like she wanted to throw up. I wasn't too excited about being there either, but Miss Rachel had made it clear that this was part of our community service. I figured the sooner we got this over with, the sooner we could get out of here.

"You ain't gotta let everybody and they mama know you don't want to be here," I whispered.

"It stinks in here," Alexis replied.

Angel walked up to the table. "You know, one day you might be old and they'll have to put you in a home. Do you want some young person coming in talking about how you stink?"

"I didn't say *they* stink," Alexis protested. "I said *it* stinks in here."

"Just go pass out the bingo cards." I fanned her away. We'd been meeting for the past month with the Good Girlz

Club and things were going a lot better than I ever imagined they would. I guess that's what happens when you tell someone all your business twice a week.

This was the first service project we had to do with the club and nobody really wanted to be here. We'd been having fun just laughing and talking at each meeting, but Rachel was adamant about us giving back to the community. I was trying my best to maintain a positive attitude today, even though I had no desire to play bingo and sing church songs with a bunch of old people.

"Aaaagggggghhhh!" The loud noise caught all of us by surprise. Everyone in the cafeteria turned toward the entrance to see what the noise was. I almost had a heart attack as I watched an elderly gray-haired man with no teeth come rolling into the cafeteria in his wheelchair. As he had to be doing about twenty-five miles an hour as he flew past me and into the wall on the other side of the cafeteria. As he hit the wall, the chair bounced back, and he bounced out and hit the floor.

Jasmine was standing in the doorway with her hand over her mouth and her eyes wide.

The elderly man pulled himself up off the floor and wobbled back into his wheelchair. "Whew, diggity, that was fun! Come on, gal, and push me again." He looked directly at Jasmine as he wheeled himself back over to her. "Come on. This time let's go all the way to the other end of the hall."

"Jasmine!" I shouted when she reached for the back of his chair. "What are you doing?"

Jasmine shrugged her shoulders. "He asked me to push him, said he wanted to go as fast as I could run."

It's a good thing Rachel had gone to the store to get

more paper cups for the breakfast we had cooked for the elderly residents. The Hester House manager was still up front, so thankfully she didn't witness that fiasco.

The man wheeled himself halfway down the hallway, before he stopped and spun his wheelchair around. "Come on, gal, what you waiting on? Just call me Evel Kneivel." He gave a hearty laugh, his toothless mouth wide open.

"What?" Jasmine said. "Y'all said we were here to entertain the residents. I'm entertaining the residents."

"Jasmine, no," Alexis said.

Jasmine let out a long breath. "Fine. Mr. O'Ray, my friends here won't let me push you anymore."

"Huh?" He was visibly upset. "Why you gotta be spoiling all my fun?" he said as he wheeled back over to us.

"Mr. O'Ray," Alexis said as she stepped closer to him, "that is a very dangerous game you and Jasmine are playing."

"How old you is, gal?" Mr. O'Ray asked.

"Sixteen," Alexis responded.

"Well, Miss Sixteen-Year-Old, I'm a very dangerous man." Mr. O'Ray winked one eye. "Come see me in about two years and I'll show you."

"Excuse me?" Alexis took a step back.

"I didn't stutter. Gimme a kiss," he said, puckering his wrinkled old lips.

I had to fight back a laugh because Alexis looked like she was going to be sick.

Before Alexis could respond, Rachel walked up and grabbed the back of his wheelchair. "Mr. O'Ray, ain't nobody about to kiss you. Especially my *underage* young girls."

Mr. O'Ray giggled. "Well then, you give me a kiss."

"I'm not kissing you, either. Come on, let's go play

bingo." Rachel pushed him over to a table. We followed, and within minutes were playing games with the residents.

After several games of bingo, and much to Jasmine's dismay, we sang church songs to the senior citizens before calling it a day.

"That was fun," Angel said as we made our way back out to the church van.

"Yeah, we need to come hang out with old people every day," Jasmine said flatly.

I looked at her like she'd lost her mind. "Are you serious?"

"Of course not," Jasmine replied.

"I don't know, I had fun. At first I didn't think I would, but the games were fun. I never got to know my grandma and it wasn't so bad," Alexis said.

"Well, I get enough of old people with my granny. I don't need any more in my life," Jasmine laughed as we climbed in the van.

Rachel was still talking to someone from the Hester House, but she'd given me the keys to start the van. I did, then turned the radio on.

"Shake that laffy taffy," I sang along with the song on 104.9.

Angel started bobbing her head, and even though she was off beat, we all encouraged her.

"Go, Angel, shake that laffy taffy," we sang. Angel punched her fists out in front of her, rose up off the seat, and started trying to shake her behind.

That had to be the funniest stuff I'd ever seen. She must've been doing the Weyoncé dance or something because that dang sure wasn't anything remotely close to what Beyoncé does.

"Oh, my God, you so can not dance," I said, laughing.

Angel kept dancing. "Don't hate the playa, hate the game."

"You need to hate those busted moves you've got," Jasmine said with a smile.

Alexis shook her head. "The sad part is she really thinks she's doing something."

Angel continued to dance and stopped only when she turned her head and saw Rachel staring at her through the car window. "Angel, I didn't know you had it in you," Rachel said as she opened the car door.

"She doesn't." Jasmine giggled.

Angel eased back down in the seat as Rachel slid into the van and turned down the radio. "I'm so glad you girls are having a good time." The laughter in the car died down. "I was worried that you all wouldn't ever get along," she said as we pulled out of the parking lot.

"After we got some people to stop being so difficult, we just kinda clicked." I turned around and looked in the backseat.

"Why you looking at me?" Jasmine snapped.

"I just looked in the back." I smiled. "That's your guilty conscience."

"Maybe you've even forged friendships that will last a lifetime," Rachel said.

"A lifetime?" Jasmine joked. "Maybe for the next two weeks, but a lifetime is a long time to have to watch Angel dance off beat, Camille boss people around, and Alexis paint her nails."

Alexis playfully pushed her shoulder. "And don't forget, have you be so nice."

"Girl, I put the *n* in nice," Jasmine said. "Tell her, Miss Rachel. I'm the nicest person you know."

Rachel eyed Jasmine in the rearview mirror. "Now, you know I'm a God-fearing woman. I'm not about to sit up here and tell a lie the day before Sunday."

"Here we go with the jokes," Jasmine said as she leaned back in the seat.

My expression turned serious. "Thank you, Miss Rachel. I think I speak for all of us when I say that. We really enjoy being a part of the Good Girlz Club, even though we may not always act like it." I was trying to figure out if I should say what else was on my mind. I decided to go ahead. "You know I go to court on Monday and I'm supposed to tell the judge whether I want to continue in your program. At first I had planned to tell her yes just because I knew that was what I was supposed to say. But now, I can honestly say I'll tell her I'm continuing because I really do love it."

Rachel looked so proud, I couldn't help but smile. Heck, I was proud myself because never in a million years did I ever think I'd actually like being in the Good Girlz group.

14

Angel

It had been three days since the last Good Girlz meeting and I was really looking forward to meeting with the girls again. Don't ask me why. Maybe being pregnant has got me all touchy-feely.

Rachel paired us up and told us to keep in touch outside the group. Thankfully, she'd put me with Camille. I wasn't about to call Jasmine and let her bite my head off. Me and Camille had talked last night for almost an hour. I think even she was shocked by how easily we'd opened up to each other.

I touched my chest as I felt another shortness of breath. This stupid asthma was gon' drive me crazy. I was on the bus now on the way to my mother's house to get my medication. I've had asthma since I was a little girl, but it only started flaring up about a year ago.

Part of me really wanted to go home for good, not just to get my medication. I was tired of sleeping on Rosario's living room floor. Rosario has four kids and a live-in boyfriend and they all stayed in a two-bedroom apartment. And that pervert of a boyfriend Rosario had was always creeping in the living room in the middle of the night. He would just stand there staring at me, making me very uncomfortable. Plus, my back was starting to hurt. Yep, it was time to go. But the only place to go was back to my mother's house. I didn't have any other relatives in town. With the exception of some distant cousins in California, most of my family was in Mexico.

Since my dad was arrested when I was just a baby, my mother spent her days working as a librarian at the Houston Public Library and her nights selling newspaper subscriptions just trying to make ends meet.

It had been nearly a month since I left home. My mother had tried everything under the sun to talk to me, but I simply couldn't face her, let alone bring myself to admit I was pregnant. You'd have to know my mother. She's soft-spoken and has a way of making you feel like dirt just by staring at you. She'd had a fit when I left and had even threatened to drag me back home, but Rosario had convinced her that I would just leave again.

It was only a block from the bus stop to my mother's house. Once I made my way onto the porch, I took a deep breath, leaned in, and pushed the doorbell. It took a few minutes, but my mother finally swung the door open.

"Mija!" she cried as she took me into her arms. She squeezed me so tightly I could barely breathe. "Please tell me you are coming home. Whatever is wrong, we can work it out."

I fought back the tears as I pulled myself from my mother's embrace. "Hi, Mami." My mother was a short, heavyset woman with olive-colored skin and wavy hair. It was naturally red, but she colored it dark brown, claiming that the red made her look "too worldly."

"I've been so worried." She stepped aside. "Come in, please. I've been praying and praying. I knew you'd come home."

I walked into the living room, trying to make sure I kept my purse in front of my stomach.

"How'd you get here? Where's your stuff?" my mother asked as she closed the door.

"I caught the bus. And I just came for my asthma medication." I hadn't been there two minutes and I felt horrible. I couldn't even look my mother in the eyes.

"No, *mija*." She rubbed my cheeks. "This has gone on too long. We must talk about what is wrong. And don't tell me it's nothing. I will not let you leave again."

She took my hands, leaned back, and stared at me. My mother must have a direct line with God or something because she has a way of seeing through anything, which is why I wouldn't raise my eyes to look at her.

"Mami." I struggled to get the words out. I needed to tell her something so she wouldn't worry. I was just about to speak when I looked up and caught her staring at my stomach, her eyes wide as saucers.

"Oh. My. God," my mother whispered as she dropped my hands. "Are you pregnant?"

I didn't know what to say. I knew my stomach was getting big, but I had worn a baggy shirt thinking it would disguise it.

My mother put one hand to her mouth and reached out with the other hand and touched my stomach. "Ay. No, God. *Por favor*, no."

I moved her hand. "Mami, please let me explain." I didn't even know how I could explain anything, but I just knew I couldn't stand the look of horror on my mother's face.

She just continued to shake her head. "No, no, no. You would not do this to me. As hard as I've worked to give you a better life, you would not do this to me. You promised me you would wait until you were married to give yourself to someone. I know you did not break your promise to me. I just know it."

My mother backed up, bumping into the end table and nearly tripping. She steadied herself, then grabbed her Bible off the table, where it had been lying open, and shook it at me. "I know you did not betray me or God like this!"

I glanced down at the beat-up hardwood floor. "I'm sorry, Mami. I made a huge mistake."

"Look at you." My mother shook her head as tears ran down her cheeks. "*Soy tan disappointed en usted. Por favor, Dios, por qué.* Why, my child, why?"

"Mami, I'm sorry I've disappointed you." I played with the strap on my belt, trying to get my words out. I wished I could just disappear.

My mother grabbed her chest like she was having a heart attack. "Lord, help my child." She dropped to her knees and began uttering prayers in Spanish.

I wanted to kick myself for coming here. I should've just taken my chances with my asthma. Better yet, I should've run away when I had the chance. That's what I was doing when I stopped at the church the night of that first Good Girlz meeting.

I grabbed some of the medication I kept in the living room, then eased out the front door. My mother didn't even notice, she was so wrapped up in her prayers.

I began walking down the street, heading to the bus stop to go back to Zion Hill. This was absolutely, positively the worst day of my life. And as long as I lived, I'd never forget that sad and disappointed look on my mother's face.

15

Camille

The guy sitting next to me looked like he had just come from shooting twelve people. The girl on the other side of me wouldn't quit bragging about how she cut her boyfriend when she caught him cheating. I felt like I was in some bad prison movie.

I could not believe I was sitting up in court like a common criminal. I was missing school to sit up with drug dealers, thieves, and murderers—all waiting to go before the judge and plead their cases.

"Camille Simone Harris," the bailiff called.

I stood up. "Right here."

"Please step forward."

I made my way up front, my mother close on my heels.

"You may approach the bench," the judge said.

Me and my mom both eased toward the bench. "Camille Simone Harris, I have reviewed your case and talked with Rachel Adams at the community service organization. It is my understanding that you have been following the terms of your release—"

"Yes, Your Honor," my mother interrupted the judge. "She's a good girl and she does what she's supposed to, except—"

The judge held up her hand. "Excuse me. Mrs. Harris, right?"

My mother nodded.

"I'm allowing you to be here for support, but I prefer to speak with your daughter directly."

My mother lowered her head and stepped back. "I'm sorry."

"Now," the judge said, turning her attention back to me. "I hope I am not being foolish when I say that I do believe you had no knowledge that Mr. Lee was a fugitive from justice. So my only requirement is that you continue to be an active participant of the Good Girlz Club. It's a phenomenal program that I believe will help keep you on the straight and narrow. If you complete the program, I will dismiss the charges. If I find that you are not participating, you will come back before me—and I assure you, you don't want that. Do I make myself clear?"

"Very," I replied softly. My heart seemed to drop with relief. I never really thought I'd have to do any hard time, but I was worried the judge might try to make an example of me. Now, I could breathe a whole lot easier.

"And Camille." The judge softened her tone. "I implore you to be wary of the company you keep. You're free to go."

My mother let out a loud sigh of relief as she clutched her chest. I ignored her and flashed a smile at the judge as my mother pulled me into an embrace.

We walked out of the courtroom, both of us with huge smiles on our faces. "You need to drop to your knees now and give thanks that you aren't doing any hard time," my mother said as soon as we were out of the courtroom.

Not even my mother could spoil my mood right now. "You're right, Mom. We'll say a special prayer tonight."

That seemed to make her happy. She hugged me one more time. "I'm going to run to the ladies' room," she said as she let me go. "I'll be right back."

I was still smiling as I watched my mother walk off. I had hoped for the best and that's just what I got. Completing this program would be a snap. Even though I didn't really like sharing my business, it wasn't all that bad. And it sure beat jail. My thoughts were interrupted by a deep female voice calling my name.

"Excuse me, were you talking to me?" I didn't recognize the girl. She was about five-foot-four, with thick hips and legs. She had on bright orange capris and a baby-doll shirt. Her blond braids were pulled up into a ponytail on the top of her head.

"Yo' name is Camille, ain't it?" The girl was smacking gum like it was the last piece she'd ever chew.

"Yes, and you would be?" I asked.

"LaShay. I'm Keith's girlfriend."

I felt my heart drop.

"Let me get something straight with you," LaShay said as she wiggled her neck. "Keith is my man. Always has been, always will be. I got his baby and you can't compete with that."

I stared at the girl. What had Keith ever seen in her? She was ghetto with a capital *G*. I wanted to slap her and tell her Keith would be behind bars for a very long time. The last thing she needed to worry about was me trying to get back with him.

"Whatever," I replied as I stepped around the girl.

LaShay grabbed my arm. "Don't let me see your name up on no visiting list trying to go see him."

"You have got to be kidding me," I said as I jerked my arm away.

"You don't want to mess with me," LaShay threatened. Although LaShay looked like she was straight from the hood, I wasn't scared. Much. Besides, there were cops all over the courthouse. I didn't think LaShay would be stupid enough to try something with me.

"You need to be mad at your so-called boyfriend. I didn't know about you. He did, and still tried to get with me. But believe me when I say you don't ever have to worry about me again because there ain't nothing Keith can do for me but leave me alone."

As if on cue, Keith came shuffling down the hall, shackled at the hands and feet. Armed guards were on both sides of him. Another guard walked behind them. LaShay cut her eyes at me before racing over to hug Keith.

"Ma'am, you need to step back," one of the guards said.

"Baby, I'm right here." She rubbed his face like she was trying to wipe something off. "I'll be right there as you go in front of the judge. Know that I got your back. Me and your baby miss you so much."

I knew that act was all for me. Even though it hurt to see Keith all chained up, it was just what I needed to realize what a mistake I'd made. Keith caught my eye and smiled.

"What up, shorty?"

I stared at him. No this fool didn't have the audacity to speak to me like nothing was wrong.

"Why you speaking to her?" LaShay pouted.

Keith ignored LaShay and scooted closer to me. "Look here, I'm sorry about the trouble I got you into. Hopefully, you'll let me make it up to you when I get out." I wanted to slap that sexy smirk off his face. I didn't get a chance to because my mother came out of the bathroom, and the next thing I knew she was swinging her purse, hitting Keith upside the head.

"You got my baby in all that trouble!" she yelled as she swung her big black bag at him again. "You no-good, carjacking thug!"

Keith shielded his head as the deputies grabbed my mother and pulled her off of him.

"Crazy old bat," Keith muttered as the deputies dragged him away.

I couldn't help but smile as my mother brushed down her skirt, grabbed my hand, and strutted off with her head held high.

16

Camille

"So you actually saw him at court?" Alexis was all ears as we sat at The Golden Corral, where we were holding our meeting. So far, only me, Alexis, and Angel had arrived.

"Girl, yes. And his baby mama." I smiled. I still couldn't believe how quickly I had made friends with the girls. Besides Melanie and Tonya, I didn't have too many friends.

"I hope you told him off," Alexis said as she took a bite of her salad.

"I didn't have to. My mom stepped in and commenced to beating him with her bag."

"You're kidding!" Both Alexis and Angel cracked up laughing.

"Hey, what's so funny?" Jasmine asked as she walked up to the table. "I know y'all betta not be talking about me."

Everyone turned to Jasmine.

I stopped laughing. "Good grief, girl. Would you chill out? Ain't nobody talking about you."

"Yeah, we were talking about Camille's boyfriend," Angel interjected.

"Ex-boyfriend," I corrected.

"What about him?" Jasmine asked as she plopped down in a seat next to Alexis.

"Camille saw him in court," Angel said.

"Oh, did you bust him in his jaw?" Jasmine asked.

I looked at her to see if she was serious. She was. "Is that your answer to everything?"

Jasmine just shrugged and grabbed a plate. "That's what I would've done," she said as she got up and headed to the buffet table.

"How'd you get here? Did you come with Miss Rachel?" Alexis asked as we got up and followed Jasmine to refill our plates.

"Naw, I caught the bus," Jasmine replied.

"The bus?" Alexis said with her nose turned up.

"Did I stutter? My Benz is in the shop this week." Jasmine rolled her eyes and walked away.

Five minutes later we were back at the table.

"So finish your story about Keith," Angel begged.

I stuffed a piece of bread in my mouth and took my time chewing. I was messing with them since I knew they were anxious to hear all the dirt. "I told you. I saw him, my mama jumped on him, his baby mama flipped out. End of story."

"I would've had to go off on him," Jasmine said.

"Yeah, like you did C.J., huh." I smirked.

Jasmine sat up and narrowed her eyes at me.

Both Alexis and Angel looked back and forth between us. "Uh, somebody want to tell us what's going on?" Alexis said.

I smiled. "Yeah, Jasmine, you want to tell them what's going on?"

Jasmine poked her lip out, then started back eating. "Ain't nothing going on," she said with a mouth full of food.

"Ewww, can you chew that first," Alexis said. She turned to me. "Who is C.J.?"

Jasmine shot me a mean look, which I ignored. "This guy at my school who likes Jasmine. And even though she's trying to act like she doesn't, I think she likes him, too."

"I do not!" Jasmine protested.

"What's the big deal?" Alexis said. "You're practically grown. You're fifteen and you act like you're in elementary school. What's wrong with liking boys?"

"I don't like boys," Jasmine said through clenched teeth.

"Then do you like girls?" I joked.

Jasmine pointed her fork at me. "Don't make me cut you." She turned to Alexis and Angel, who looked like they were waiting for an answer. "Don't make me cut all of y'all! Of course I don't like girls. I just ain't got time for no silly boy."

I leaned in and whispered, "Have you ever had a boyfriend before, Jasmine?" Jasmine was the only one who hadn't really opened up. "Or better yet, you ever kissed a boy?"

Jasmine looked at us like we were all crazy. "Why are y'all all up in my business?" She grabbed her roll and took a bite out of it. She chomped slowly while everyone stared at her.

"I don't know what y'all looking at," Jasmine said. "I'm not going to answer that question."

"Why not?" Alexis asked. "I'm not ashamed to say I've never had sex. I'm going to wait until I'm married." She held her head high. Me and Jasmine groaned and rolled our eyes.

"And we know Camille has had a boyfriend," Alexis continued. "And Angel, well, we know Angel has had sex."

We all busted out laughing, except Angel, who was staring at the front door.

"Angel, don't get mad. We were just messing with you," Alexis said.

"No, it's . . . it's not that. That's Marcus." She pointed to a guy who had his arm draped around a petite, blond-haired girl who was giggling at something he'd whispered in her ear. Angel's eyes watered up. "I'm ready to go."

"But we're still waiting on Miss Rachel," Alexis protested.

"Yeah," Jasmine added. "And she has to pay for our food 'cause I sho' ain't got no money."

Marcus leaned in and kissed the girl on the lips.

"I wonder if he's feeding her the same lines he fed me," Angel whispered, more to herself than to anyone else.

I looked back and forth between Marcus and the girl and Angel. I could see Angel was truly hurting and don't ask me why, but I felt the need to do something. "I don't know, let's go ask him." Before anyone could say anything, I had jumped up and was walking over to where they stood.

"What's going on, Marcus?" I stood with my hands on my hips.

Marcus stopped giggling and he and the girl stared at me. "Do I know you?" he asked.

"No, boy," I said, slapping his arm. "But you do know my friend." I turned and waved toward the table. "Angel, come here."

A stunned Angel didn't move. Jasmine grabbed her arm and pulled her out of the chair. She all but dragged her over and pushed her next to me.

"You know my girl, Angel, right?"

Marcus's eyes had gotten big. The girl was looking at him for answers.

"Pardon my rudeness," I said to the girl. I stuck out my hand. "I'm Camille. And this is Jasmine." I pointed to Jasmine, then to Alexis, who was now standing next to Jasmine. "That's Alexis." I grabbed Angel's hand and pulled her in front of me. "And this is Angel. And, oh yeah"—I put my hand on Angel's stomach—"this is Marcus's baby."

The girl's eyes grew huge as she stepped away from Marcus. "What?"

"Baby, let me explain." Marcus was flustered and could barely get his words out. "That ain't my kid. I don't know what they're talking about."

The girl stared at him with her mouth hanging open. "Marcus, we've been together over a year. How is she pregnant?" the girl asked.

"I told you, that ain't mine. She been with everybody and now she trying to pin that on me!"

The girl crossed her arms. "Oh, but does that everybody include you?"

"I—I didn't mean that. I—I was just saying—"

"Well, we see you have some things you need to work out," I interrupted. I was trying my best not to laugh. That's what he got. "We'll be going. Oh, and Marcus, Angel will be getting in touch with you about child support. You two enjoy your dinner."

I sashayed back to the table with all three of the girls close behind me.

We all sat in silence for a few minutes before Jasmine started cracking up. "Okay, that was off the chain, Camille. I didn't know you had it in you."

"Me, either," Alexis laughed.

"Thank you," Angel mumbled. She still seemed sad. "I'm glad you stood up to him, especially since I can't seem to do it."

I placed my hand on top of Angel's hands. "It's a lot easier to do when it's not your own man." I thought about my own day in court and wished I'd been able to stand up to Keith like that.

17

Camille

Reverend Adams pounded his fist on the podium as he talked about people not listening to God. He had caught my attention when he'd said that because I sure wasn't listening. I was sitting on a middle pew trying to figure out how we had ended up at Bible study.

When Rachel had shown up at the restaurant, we'd filled her in on what happened. She'd laughed with us, paid for our dinners, then told us she had a surprise for us. We'd piled into Alexis's car and followed Rachel back to the church. I was definitely surprised when Rachel led us into Bible study.

I wasn't a heathen by any means, but I wasn't trying to be sitting up in church on a Wednesday night, especially when *America's Next Top Model* was due on any minute. But what was I supposed to say?

I leaned in toward Jasmine, who looked just as disinterested. "Touch Alexis," I whispered.

Jasmine nudged Alexis, who was actually dosing off. Alexis jumped, and Jasmine and I had to cover our mouths to keep from laughing.

"Are you ready to go?" I whispered.

Alexis nodded. "But we can't leave yet," she whispered back.

I sighed and leaned back. I probably should've been listening, but my mind kept replaying my day in court. Why was I still thinking about Keith? Even better, why was I letting him get to me? Keith was a dog and the sooner I got over him, the better off I'd be.

I looked up and saw that Rev. Adams was wrapping up. I eyed my watch. It was almost eight o'clock. I'd missed *Top Model* and tonight they were cutting it down to the last two model wannabes.

"I don't understand why we needed to be here," I whispered to Jasmine as Rachel walked up to the front of the church. "Besides, I thought you were supposed to *teach* at Bible study. He's been preaching twenty minutes."

Jasmine fought back a yawn. "Preaching, teaching. It's not like you would've listened either way."

I sat back in my seat. She had a point there.

"Brothers and Sisters," Rachel began. "I know you all have things you need to be doing, but I wanted to take a moment to introduce you to my girls tonight." She motioned for us to stand, which we did.

"These young ladies are members of our church's Good Girlz Club and they are already on their way to making the church proud." Rachel beamed like a proud mama. "They'll be formally introduced at a future Sunday service, but I wanted you to at least know who they are."

All four of us smiled as people began clapping. After Rev. Adams dismissed everyone, we began mingling with people from the Bible study class. All the members were so friendly that I almost felt bad about being so ready to go. Alexis and Jasmine seemed to be enjoying the attention as well. I looked around the room for Angel. She was nowhere to be found.

I excused myself from the elderly woman who was trying to fix me up with her grandson, some bug-eyed nerd
she'd pulled out a picture of and showed me. I made my
way out into the foyer. It wasn't like Angel to leave without
saying something.

I spotted her sitting on a bench at the end of the foyer.
"Hey, girl, what are you doing out here all by yourself?"

Angel raised her head. Her eyes looked red, like she'd
been crying. "Just thinking."

"About what?" I sat down next to her.

"All these people . . . they make me feel . . . I don't know,
so loved. And then I felt my baby kick," Angel said softly.

"Wow." I reached out and touched Angel's stomach.
"That's cool."

"Really, it's not. I got scared. Then that started me
thinking about what I'm going to do when the baby gets
here. I have nowhere to go." Angel sniffed loudly.

"Do you think there's a chance that your mother will
forgive you?"

"Let me put it this way: I have a bigger chance of win-
ning the lottery."

"You know what? You're still her child. I bet if you go
over there and beg for her forgiveness she'll hear you out."

"I don't think so."

"What about your sister?" I asked. I really felt bad for
Angel. I couldn't imagine dealing with something so deep.

"She'll help, but she has her hands full already. Plus, I
don't like her boyfriend."

I leaned back against the bench. "Dang. This is too
much drama."

"Tell me about it," Angel mumbled.

"What are you all doing out here?" Alexis was standing

in the doorway of the sanctuary. Jasmine was next to her. "Are you ready to go?"

Angel started laughing and everybody stared at her like she'd lost her mind. Alexis and Jasmine looked at me. "What is wrong with her?" Jasmine asked.

I shrugged, wondering if she'd flipped out.

"Yeah," Angel said, wiping the tears that had started flowing through her laughter. "I'm ready to go. Problem is, I have no place *to* go. I mean, I could go back to my sister's, but I know I'm wearing out my welcome there." She laughed some more.

Alexis sat on Angel's other side. "Oh, Angel. I'm so sorry. You can come to my house. You know my mom doesn't care."

Angel abruptly stopped laughing and wiped her face again. "And what about the next night? And the night after that? You think your parents would go for that? I don't think so," Angel said without giving her time to answer.

I rubbed Angel's arm. "Why don't you go home? I can't believe I'm saying this, but talk this through with your mother. Try, please. We'll go with you, won't we?" I looked at Alexis and Jasmine and they both nodded.

"I told you, I can't go home," Angel said.

"Why not?" I asked.

Angel looked at us like she really didn't have an answer. She finally let a small smile cross her face. "Fine, I'll try to talk to her. But only if you all go with me. And only if you promise not to talk about how crazy my mother is afterward."

"Girl, please," I laughed. "I think motherhood makes you crazy or something, because as far as I'm concerned, everybody's mama is crazy, especially mine."

"Nope, sorry, I think mine has you beat," Alexis said as she stood up. "She put the *drama* in 'drama queen.'"

The sound of a blaring horn made us all look outside the church's front door. An elderly woman was sitting in a beat-up Lincoln Town Car. She had pink rollers all over her head and she wore what looked like a tattered bathrobe. Jasmine pushed the church doors open.

"Come on here, gal. I gots to get home. You know it's past my bedtime!" the woman shouted.

Jasmine inhaled deeply. "I'm coming, Granny." She turned back toward us. "Shoot, try having a crazy mama *and* a crazy grandma under one roof. That's my life. So I think I got y'all beat. 'Bye." Jasmine shook her head as she walked toward the car.

All three of us laughed as we waved to Jasmine.

"Meet us tomorrow after school so we can go over Angel's house!" I called out.

Jasmine nodded her head and got in the car. Before they drove away, we heard Jasmine's grandmother loudly proclaim, "Don't think I'm driving you nowhere tomorrow. You ain't Miss Daisy."

Me, Alexis, and Angel couldn't help but laugh as her grandmother drove off.

18

Angel

Camille and Alexis each gripped one of my hands tightly. If it weren't for them, I'm sure I would have turned and bolted, saying forget this whole thing.

"Come on, girl. Just talk to her. She's your mother, she doesn't hate you," Jasmine said as she led the way to my mom's front door. She reached up and rang the doorbell.

I took a deep breath and eyed the door.

"Who is it?" my mother called out.

"It's me, Mami," I responded.

Alexis leaned in and whispered to Camille, "I think Spanish is so cool. I want to learn how to speak it."

"Would you shut up? We're trying to handle some business here," she hissed.

Alexis stuck out her lips in a pout.

My mother didn't say anything as she opened the door. She stepped out on the porch and closed the door behind her. "Angel!" She gave me a huge hug. "I have been worried about you. If it weren't for your sister, I wouldn't know whether you were dead or alive." She eyed Alexis, Jasmine, and Camille.

"These are my friends." My voice was shaking. "May I come in and talk to you?"

My mother softly stroked my face. "I do want to talk to you." She looked toward the door. "Now's just not a good time."

Huh? I knew she'd been dying to get me to talk, she worried Rosario enough. Now, she was talking about it wasn't a good time? "Please, Mami."

Just then the front door opened and a pretty, dark-haired woman peeked out. "Mrs. Lopez, I'm sorry to interrupt, but Donald and I really must get going." The woman's eyes made their way over to me. "Oh, my. You must be Angel. You are the spitting image of your mother."

I looked at my mother, who suddenly had a terrified look.

The woman poked her head back in the house and yelled, "Donald! Sweetie, come here. It's Angel."

My mother tried to go back into the house. "Mrs. Hartford, now is not the time. We must do this later."

"Nonsense," the woman said, stepping out onto the porch and around my mother. She looked me up and down. "My, my, my. You are beautiful. And look at your cute little belly." The woman reached out and rubbed my stomach, which was now showing just a little.

A man, who must've been Donald, stepped out on the porch.

"Isn't she beautiful?" the woman said, never taking her eyes off of me.

"That she is," Donald said as he extended his hand. "Hi, I'm Donald Hartford."

I looked at my mother again. Who were these people, how did they know me, and why were they rubbing all over my stomach? My mother looked away. No answers there.

"It's nice to meet you," I mumbled to them. "But who are you?"

Both of them smiled widely. The woman answered, "Oh, we're the couple that's here to see about adopting your baby."

I swear I was about to pass out right on the front porch.

My mother stepped in before I could say anything. "The Hartfords are a respectable couple who really want a child. I just asked them over to talk to them about the idea."

I stared at my mother as my eyes filled with tears. I couldn't believe her. Adoption? My mother had just up and decided to give my baby away without even talking to me about it? "Mami, what are you doing?"

"I'm just looking at options, that's all," my mother said as she tried to flash the Hartfords a reassuring smile.

"No! It's my baby! I won't give her away!" I turned and raced off the porch. I didn't know where I was going, but I had to get out of there. I could hear Camille, Jasmine, and Alexis running after me.

"Hey, wait up," Alexis called as I stomped down the street.

"Where are you going, Angel?" Camille called out. "Would you please stop? We drove here, remember?"

I stopped. I wasn't thinking clearly. "Are you okay?" Camille asked as they caught up with me.

I shook my head. "I can't just give my baby to strangers."

"Sweetie, you don't have to do anything you don't want to," Alexis said.

I felt an asthma attack coming on and fought to get my breathing under control. "But it looks like she's already promised my child to them."

"Then she will just have to unpromise them," Jasmine said.

"I'm underage. Can't she just take my child?" My breaths felt like they were getting shorter and shorter.

"Not if she doesn't want to end up on *America's Most Wanted*," Jasmine said.

I closed my eyes and managed to get my breath back. No one said anything, but I'm sure I looked like an idiot standing there with my eyes squeezed shut, holding my chest.

When I felt like I could finally breathe again, I opened my eyes and stared at my new friends. "I need to figure all of this out. I'm sorry." I turned and took off down the street before any of them could protest.

19

Camille

*M*y heart sank as I looked around the room. Angel was always the first one at the meetings and she was nowhere to be found. I was definitely starting to get worried. It had been three days and I hadn't heard from her. That was unusual because if I didn't see Angel in person, she always managed to find a way to call and check in.

"Ummm, Miss Rachel," I said when I noticed Rachel about to start the meeting. "I'm just wondering, have you heard from Angel?"

"No, I was going to ask you girls the same thing." A worried look crossed Rachel's face. "This isn't like her. And Jasmine isn't here, either."

No sooner had Rachel said her name then Jasmine came bursting in the door. "Y'all are not going to believe this!"

"What?" I was the first one out of my seat.

"Angel tried to kill Marcus!" Jasmine shouted.

"What?" everyone said at the same time.

"My brother knows Marcus and he was hanging out at the basketball court when Angel showed up after school, talking about she needed to get out of town and she needed some money. She told Marcus that he needed to be a man and help her out." Jasmine was out of breath.

"Angel said that?" Alexis asked.

"That's what my brother said." Jasmine rushed her words out. "Anyway, Marcus told her to beat it and she lost it. She picked up a broken bottle, pushed him up against a wall, and held the glass to his neck!"

"Where is she now?" Rachel asked.

"He gave her all the money in his pocket. My brother said it was about fifty bucks and she told him he'd never have to worry about her again because she was heading to California," Jasmine said.

Rachel looked like she was trying her best to stay calm. "California?"

"Does she know anyone in California? How is she going to take care of her baby?" Alexis started pacing back and forth.

"I don't know all of that," Jasmine replied.

Alexis stopped pacing and turned toward Rachel. "Oh, my God, Miss Rachel. We've got to find her."

"How?" Jasmine asked.

"Come on," Rachel said as she grabbed her purse off the floor. "She doesn't have a car. She couldn't have had enough money to fly. Maybe she's going on the bus."

Alexis grabbed her purse as well. "The bus station is downtown. I'll drive."

"No, girls, you'd better let me drive," Rachel said.

Fifteen minutes later, we pulled up in front of the Greyhound bus station. Alexis looked around, a disgusted look on her face.

"What? You think you too good to be at a bus station?" Jasmine snapped.

Alexis rolled her eyes and started to speak but Rachel jumped in before either of them could say another word. "Don't you two start."

"Yeah," I echoed. "This is about Angel." Alexis and Jasmine immediately looked apologetic.

"I'm going in," Jasmine said as she climbed out of the passenger seat.

I quickly followed. Alexis hesitated, but then followed as well.

"I'm going to find a parking space. I'll be right in," Rachel called out behind them.

We ran to catch up to Jasmine, who was already making her way into the station.

Once inside we began looking around the crowded bus station. "Do you see her?" Jasmine asked frantically.

"No," I replied. "Let's split up."

We went our separate ways, but after five minutes, we still weren't having any luck. "I'm going to ask the ticket lady," I said when we met back up. I made my way up to the counter. "Excuse me, ma'am." The clerk was smacking on a wad of gum while she talked on the telephone. She held up one finger to let me know she'd be with me in a minute.

"Girl, no he didn't," the clerk laughed into the phone. I couldn't believe this woman. I knocked on the window. "Excuse me, I just have a quick question."

The woman frowned as she moved the phone to her chest. "I said, I'll be with you in a minute." She moved the phone back to her ear and started laughing again.

"This is crazy," I muttered. I raised my voice to the

woman. "I just need to know if you've seen a pretty Hispanic teenaged girl in here in the last hour or so. She's by herself and pregnant."

The clerk exhaled loudly, then told whoever she was talking to that she'd call them back. She hung up the phone.

I sighed. "Thank you. Now, I'm looking for my friend. Her name is Angel Lopez. She's about—"

The woman cut me off. "It is the policy of Greyhound Bus services not to disclose that type of information to anyone other than law enforcement officials. I'm terribly sorry. Next!" She smirked and cocked her head.

For once, I wanted to take Jasmine's advice and bust her in her jaw. Instead, I just rolled my eyes and stomped off.

I looked around for Alexis and Jasmine. Just as I spotted them, the woman who had been behind me in the ticket line walked over and tapped me on the shoulder. "Excuse me, I don't mean to intrude, but I heard you asking the ticket agent about a young, pretty pregnant girl that you were looking for."

"Yeah, have you seen her?" I asked.

"You just missed her. I saw her get on a bus heading to Mexico about fifteen minutes ago," the woman said.

"Mexico!" I replied.

The woman nodded her head. "Poor thing looked so sad. I tried to talk to her, but she seemed like she didn't really want to be bothered."

"Oh, my God. Thank you." I shook the lady's hand, then took off back over to where Jasmine, Alexis, and now Rachel were standing.

"Any luck?" Rachel asked.

"You're not going to believe this," I said. "She's on her way to Mexico."

"Mexico!" All three of them yelled at the same time.

I pointed across the room. "That lady said Angel just left about fifteen minutes ago."

"Well, we can still catch her then," Alexis said.

Jasmine looked at Alexis like she was crazy. "How we gon' do that?" she said. "We don't know where in Mexico she was going or which way she went to get there."

"We need to at least try," Alexis pleaded. "She's all by herself. That's dangerous."

"Girls, calm down," Rachel said. She looked like she was trying to figure out what to do. "We can't go traipsing off to Mexico. We'll just have to call her mother and let her family take it from here."

"But, Miss Rachel," I said. "We're like the only family she has now."

Rachel touched my arm. "I know you are all worried about her. So am I. But there's nothing else we can do. Come on, let me get you back to the church so you can get home."

All three of us followed Rachel out in silence. I imagined Angel scared and alone on the bus. I wouldn't be able to sleep knowing she was out there by herself. I had to do something. I knew Rachel wasn't going to want to hear anything about us trying to go find Angel. But I knew we had to at least try.

Yep, as soon as Rachel dropped us off, I was hitting the road. I just hoped Alexis and Jasmine were game.

20

Camille

I felt like a special agent or something. Me, Alexis, and Jasmine were standing in the parking lot of Zion Hill. The sun had long gone down and it was pitch-black outside.

Rachel had dropped us off, promising to keep us posted. In the meantime, she was headed to Mrs. Lopez's house to break the news to her.

"Are you thinking what I'm thinking?" I asked as we stood next to Alexis's car.

"What, that we have got to find Angel?" Alexis said.

I nodded. "Y'all know Angel would do the same for us. And right about now, we're the only ones who can convince her to come back."

"Yeah, but how are we going to get to Mexico?" Jasmine asked.

"We drive," I said matter-of-factly.

"Are you on drugs?" Jasmine said.

"No, I'm dead serious. I mean, Mexico isn't that far away," I said.

"Yeah, but we don't even know what part of Mexico she's headed to." Jasmine looked at me like I was crazy. "You can't really be thinking about getting in a car and driving to Mexico."

"That's exactly what I'm thinking," I said with a mischievous grin. "Come on, it'll be fun."

Jasmine kept shaking her head. "Ain't nothing fun about driving around in the dark trying to find Mexico. And by ourselves at that? Y'all done lost your minds." She stared at us like she was waiting for someone to tell her it was all a big joke. "Don't you have to have some special papers to go to Mexico or something?" she said when no one responded. "And I ain't trying to go across the border anyway. Shoot, we mess around and they won't let us back."

"Hopefully we don't have to actually go to Mexico," I said. "You know those buses drive slow and make a hundred stops."

"So do you think we can catch her along the way?" Alexis asked. She definitely seemed down.

"Yep," I responded.

"Let's do it. We can take my car," Alexis said. "We can run by my house and look at MapQuest to get directions."

Jasmine looked like she still wasn't convinced. "Y'all, maybe we should wait and let Miss Rachel handle this. I mean, it's almost ten o'clock. We gon' get on the road by ourselves? We don't even know where she's headed."

"I told you, we'll find all of that out," I said.

"What about school tomorrow?" Jasmine asked.

"We won't die if we miss one day of school," I replied. "Besides, we may make it back before school even starts."

"We don't have any money," Jasmine protested. She seemed like she was looking for any reason not to go.

"Please. I have a credit card," Alexis replied. "You know money is not an issue."

I smiled. For once, Alexis didn't sound like she was trying to put anybody down when she talked about her money.

"Any more excuses, Jasmine?" I asked. "The more time we stand around here debating whether we should go, the farther away she's getting."

"I just don't know," Jasmine said, shaking her head.

Now I was getting frustrated. Angel was out there alone and we were sitting up here arguing. "You know what, Jasmine? You don't have to go. Me and Alexis will find Angel ourselves."

Jasmine stuck her lip out. "Why you gotta sound like that?" She hesitated. "Fine. But if my grandmother kills me, it's on y'all."

"Hopefully we'll be back before your grandmother even realizes you were gone," I said.

We piled into Alexis's car and headed to her house. On the way, I called the bus station and learned Angel's bus was headed to Matamoras, Mexico, which was right on the Texas/Mexico border.

"See, that ain't far," I said as I snapped my phone closed.

"Yeah, my mom goes shopping there sometimes," Alexis said. "It's about six hours away."

"Six hours?" Jasmine yelled.

I ignored her and looked at Alexis. "The lady on the phone said the bus was making several stops and was scheduled to be in Victoria, Texas, by one A.M."

"Well, that's where we'll catch her," Alexis said with a grin.

"Are we even sure she got on that bus?" Jasmine said. It was obvious she still wasn't feeling this idea.

"The woman at the bus station was sure she did. Plus, we just have to take a chance," I responded.

"Have y'all thought about what you'll do if you catch up with her and she doesn't want to come back?" Jasmine asked. "Are you going to beat her over the head and make her come?"

"We'll cross that bridge when we get to it," I said. "Plus, you're the beater in the group. We'll do what we gotta do." Me and Alexis laughed. Jasmine slouched in the backseat, obviously still not finding anything funny.

As Alexis made her way onto the freeway, I couldn't help but think about my mother. She was going to blow a gasket if I didn't come home. "You know, maybe we should at least call and let our moms know where we are."

"Please, I could be gone for two weeks before anyone would even notice around my house," Alexis said with a sad look on her face.

"Well, I'll call. I'm gonna tell one of my brothers 'cause I ain't about to tell my grandma," Jasmine said. She reached up for Alexis's cell phone and called her house.

After she instructed her little brother to tell her grandmother she was spending the night at my house, she handed the phone back to Alexis. "If she wakes up, I'm dead. She ain't gon' be trying to hear nothing about spending the night at somebody's house." Jasmine's tough-girl act was gone. She seemed genuinely scared.

I pulled out my own cell phone and punched in my mother's cell phone number. I knew my mother wouldn't answer her cell this late at night and I'd much rather leave a message. "Hey, Ma," I began after the tone. "Um, my friend Angel is kinda having a hard time and well, me and the other girls are gonna go help her out tonight. I'll be spending the night with her, so I'll call you tomorrow. Don't worry about me. I'll talk to you later."

I turned my phone off and snapped it closed. My mother would be calling soon because leaving a message wasn't going to fly. She'd have a hundred and one questions and I felt if I turned my phone off I wouldn't have to deal with her.

Alexis pulled up in front of her house, parking in the circular driveway. "We need to hurry up," she said as she climbed out. "I'm just going to run and get directions off MapQuest."

"Well, I need to use the restroom before we get on the road," Jasmine said as she climbed out behind her.

I followed them in as well. The huge three-story house was dark as we made our way in.

"Where's your mom?" I said as we walked into the kitchen. I looked around. The size of their kitchen didn't make any sense. It was huge. The stove was on an island in the middle of the room and the refrigerator was built into the wall. There was even a television built into the refrigerator. The house looked like something you'd see on *MTV Cribs*.

"Who knows," Alexis responded.

I followed Alexis through the kitchen into the den. I noticed a picture of an overweight girl who looked like she couldn't be more than ten or eleven. The girl wore huge glasses and had big braces.

"Oooh-weee," I said as I picked up a picture. "Is this one of your relatives? If so, y'all need to get this poor child some help."

Alexis walked over and snatched the picture out of my hands. She put the picture back on the shelf. "That's me."

"Oh, snap," I said. "What happened? You had to be almost two hundred pounds there."

"One day I'll have to tell you all about it," Alexis said as she sat down at the computer. "Right now, we've got to find Angel and that's the only thing we need to be focused on."

"Hurry up. We don't want to miss her," Jasmine said as she walked out of the bathroom.

Alexis smiled. "That's what I'm talking about. The Good Girlz to the rescue."

I laughed. Jasmine had come a long way since that first day at church. And watching Alexis and Jasmine right now, I couldn't help but feel like I'd found friends for life.

21

Camille

I might as well have been reading the world atlas because I couldn't make any sense out of the map in front of me. According to the map, we should still be on Highway 59.

I squinted up at the road sign. "So how did I get on Highway 185?"

Alexis and Jasmine were both fast asleep. Some help they were. I let out a frustrated sigh. Although Victoria was only two hours away from Houston, we'd been on the road for three and still hadn't made it there. I had to finally admit it: We were definitely lost. I focused my attention back on the map, turning it upside down to make sure I was looking at it right. I wanted to try and get back on the right track before Jasmine and Alexis woke up.

Jasmine stirred in the backseat. She yawned loudly, then said, "Are we there yet? I'm tired of riding." She stretched and looked around. "Where the heck are we?"

"We're almost there." I smashed the map down on the side of my leg.

Jasmine looked at the clock on the radio. "It's after midnight. I thought you said it only took two hours." She peered out the window. "Why are we in the woods, Camille? Where are we?"

"I don't know," I mumbled.

"Come again?" Jasmine said as she leaned forward.

I raised my voice. "I said, I don't know." No sense in acting like everything was all right anymore. We were lost, plain and simple.

"What? You mean we're lost?" Jasmine's loud voice made Alexis jump out of her sleep. She wiped the drool that was trickling down the side of her mouth.

"Huh? Wha . . . what's going on?" Alexis asked.

"Miss Bright-idea-let's-drive-to-Mexico-in-the-middle-of-the-night is lost," Jasmine snapped.

Alexis sat up. "Lost? How'd that happen?"

I pulled the crumpled map out and tossed it at Alexis. "Maybe if you two weren't so busy sleeping, you could've helped me figure out where I was going."

Alexis looked around. I'd pulled off on the side of the road. "Where are we?" She glanced down at the map. "I can't tell anything by this."

"Did you not hear me say I don't know?" I barked.

"Oh, no. Isn't this how those people came up missing in *Texas Chainsaw Massacre*?" Alexis whined.

I narrowed my eyes at Alexis. "Thanks, Alexis, for the positive thoughts. Why don't you say some more stuff to freak Jasmine out."

It was too late, Jasmine was already on a rampage. "I told y'all we didn't need to be out here. I told you, I told you, I told you! Some truck driver is going to come along, cut our heads off, and throw our bodies on the back of his truck." Jasmine slapped her forehead. "I knew I shouldn't have listened to this stupid idea."

"Would you two shut up?" I said. "We just got off track

a bit. We'll pull into the next service station and ask them which way to go."

I started the car back up and pulled out into the pitch-black street. I'd figured Jasmine would be worried, but now even Alexis was starting to look concerned.

"I don't even see a gas station," Alexis said after we'd gone a few minutes down a deserted road. She was twisting her purse straps nervously in her hands. "Can't you just go back the way we came? When did you make a wrong turn?"

"I don't know! If I knew that I wouldn't have made a wrong turn," I snapped. I was starting to get scared myself. I couldn't recall passing a single car in the last hour or so, nor had I seen any signs of life, period. I breathed a sigh of relief when I finally noticed a Phillips 66 gas station coming up. The lights were off, but I could see someone standing outside.

"We'll just pull in here and ask somebody," I said as I eased the car into the gas station. The long-haired male attendant was just closing up. He locked the door, then turned and watched our car as we pulled up.

"Excuse me," Alexis said after she rolled down her window. "Can you tell us how to get to Victoria?"

"As in Texas?" he said as he walked over to the car. His eyes seemed to light up when he leaned down and looked inside the car. "What are you beautiful girls doing out at this time of night?" His voice was raspy and he had a deep Texas twang. The way he kept licking his lips made me uneasy. He looked dirty, like he hadn't had a bath in days. Oil and dirt covered his clothes and his long, stringy blond hair looked like it was in need of a good washing.

"We're, um, on our way to Victoria," Alexis said. "And we

kinda got turned around. Can you tell us how to get back on the right freeway?" She turned to me. "Which one is it?"

I kept my eye on the man. He looked sneaky and made me nervous. "Highway 59."

He chuckled, but I didn't know what was funny. "Well, you little ladies are a long way out of the way." He stood up and looked up and down the street. "It's kind of difficult to explain. I'm heading that way. You ladies can just follow me and I'll wave to you when we get to the freeway."

"Thank you very much," Alexis said, a big smile on her face.

Alexis rolled her window up as we watched the man walk over to his car.

"He was nice," Alexis said.

Jasmine let out a long sigh. "That man is a serial killer if I ever seen one. We're as good as dead."

"Jasmine, please. Why are you being so scary?" I wasn't getting a good vibe about the guy either, but I didn't want to let Alexis and Jasmine know that.

"Because dying wasn't on my list of things to do today," Jasmine replied.

The man slowly pulled out into the street and I eased the car up behind him.

"Come on, guys, it's not like we're actually in the car with the man," Alexis said. "We're just following him to the highway, that's all."

"Can somebody pass me a pen and some paper," Jasmine said solemnly.

"For what?" I looked up in the rearview mirror.

"So I can write a good-bye letter to my family. Because we gon' die tonight. They'll probably never find our bodies," Jasmine replied.

I tried my best to ignore Jasmine as we continued following the man. After about fifteen minutes I felt myself getting even more nervous. Alexis started fidgeting in her seat. "Wow, we sure got way off track," Alexis said.

I didn't say anything. I was sure I didn't go this far out of the way. When we turned down a small dirt road, I knew the man wasn't heading anywhere near the highway.

"Oh. My. God." I looked at the two sets of headlights that were blocking the road we were headed down.

The man we were following parked, then got out and watched us. I had slowed down because this definitely wasn't right.

"Y'all, look." I pointed to the group of men who were standing outside of the parked vehicles.

Alexis's mouth dropped open. Jasmine leaned up toward the front seat and stared out the window. "Why did I listen to you guys?" she muttered.

There had to be eight men standing outside. The man from the service station started walking toward our car.

"Lock the doors," I whispered quickly. Alexis immediately pushed the lock button.

The man hit the window. "Hey, hows 'bout you ladies get out and come party with us for a little bit. We'll make sure you get back on the road in plenty of time to get where you're going."

I sat frozen. All of the men looked just as nasty as the gas station man.

Both Alexis and Jasmine seemed like they were about to lose their minds. I looked to my left and right. The street we were on was narrow, so the only option I had was to back straight up.

I took a deep breath. This was all my fault. I had to

think fast. I smiled at the man, then cracked my window. "Hey, we're all for a little fun," I said in the sweetest voice I could come up with.

The man seemed surprised.

"What are you doing?" Jasmine hissed.

I discreetly waved my hand, telling Jasmine to be quiet.

"We got a little whiskey in the car. You girls seem a little young, but I'm sure you've had whiskey before," he said.

"All the time," I laughed. I hoped my fake laugh didn't sound too fake.

"Well, why don't you ladies get on out of the car so we can, as you young 'uns like to say, get this party started," he said.

I kept my smile pasted on my face. "Party? Out here in the woods? Nah. My girls have to use the restroom and we don't go in the woods. Why don't you go see if one of your friends over there has a place we can go hang out at. We're kind of tired anyway and ready to get off the road."

The man looked at me skeptically. I flashed him an innocent look and it must have been convincing because he walked back over to the parked cars. As soon as he walked away, I eased the car into reverse, then hit the gas pedal as hard as I could. The tires screeched as I took off backward. I was like a stunt driver in the movies. The car spun around and I almost lost control, but managed to straighten up and take off. Both Alexis and Jasmine began screaming. I knew I had to tune them out and get out of there as fast as I could.

I drove a good twenty minutes before I stopped to get my bearings. I had been scared they would follow me, but when I looked around and realized no one was behind me, I relaxed a bit. Alexis and Jasmine were both quiet, their eyes wide with fear. I wanted to cry. Not only because we had narrowly escaped what could have turned into tragedy, but because I still had no idea where we were.

"Can we go home now?" Jasmine whispered. She seemed like she could barely talk.

"What about Angel?" I replied. We couldn't come this far just to turn around.

"We probably missed her by now. We tried, Camille. We really did," Jasmine said. "But we don't need to be out here by ourselves. Please, let's go home."

I hated to admit it, but Jasmine was right. I sighed, looking for road signs to figure out how to get home. I was just about to call 911 when I spotted a sign. "Look! Victoria, twenty-nine miles!"

"What?" Alexis responded. She looked at the sign. "You mean we were this close?"

I wanted to cry for real this time. But this time it was tears of joy. I looked back at Jasmine. "We're almost there now. Can we at least try and get Angel?"

Jasmine kept her jaw tight before responding. "Fine. But only if you promise, no more bright ideas."

"I promise." I smiled. I felt renewed as I followed the signs to Victoria.

22

Camille

$\mathcal{W}$e pulled up into the gas station/bus stop in Victoria. It was just after one in the morning. Jasmine and Alexis must have been too wired to go back to sleep because they both sat straight as a board in their seats.

Alexis yawned and stretched. "This has been a crazy night. And boy am I tired."

"Think of how I feel. Until we got lost, you and Jasmine had been asleep the whole way," I joked, trying to lighten the mood.

"Unh-unh. I drove, too," Alexis protested.

"Yeah, to the other side of Houston. Then you started hollerin' about you were too sleepy to drive. I'll be right back." I shook my head as I got out of the car and walked inside the store. "Hello," I said to the clerk. "Has the bus from Houston gotten here yet?"

"Nope, it's due in about thirty minutes," the clerk replied.

"Okay, thanks." I made my way back out to the car. "Good, we didn't miss the bus. It hasn't made it here yet," I said as I climbed back in. "It's due in about thirty minutes."

"I hope she's on it. We get her and get our tails back to Houston," Jasmine said.

"Guys, I'm sorry." I never imagined we would've had such a difficult time catching up with Angel.

"Don't worry about it," Alexis said. "At least you got us out safely."

"Yeah, because if that man had killed me, I would've had to come back from the dead to kill you." Jasmine finally smiled as she leaned her head back against the seat.

I giggled and leaned back, too. We sat taking in the quiet and the next thing I knew, all three of us had dozed off. Instinct made me pop up about forty-five minutes later. I glanced over to see the big gray bus parked in front of the gas station. I shook Jasmine and Alexis. "Wake up. The bus is here. Let's go."

It took a minute for everything to register, but when it did, Alexis and Jasmine jumped out of the car and followed me inside.

"Do you see her?" Alexis asked as she caught up with me.

We looked around the small station. Angel was nowhere in sight.

"Where could she be? I hope that lady knew what she was talking about." I prayed that we hadn't gone on a wild-goose chase. I turned to look around the station one more time. I was just about to walk away when I spotted Angel wobbling out of the ladies' room. "Angel!"

Angel looked up and frowned when she spotted us. "Camille! What are you doing here? What are you all doing here?"

Alexis ran over and hugged Angel. "We were so worried about you."

Angel still had a confused look on her face. "Are you guys alone?" she asked as she glanced around the station.

"Yes, we drove down here trying to find you," Alexis said.

"By yourselves?" Angel was obviously astonished.

"Yes, we were worried about you being out here by yourself," I said.

"Wow. I can't believe you went through all of that for me." Angel hesitated before speaking again. "But I hope you didn't come here to try and talk me into coming back. I'm not letting them take my baby." She rubbed her stomach. "I mean, I know I messed up and all, but I can accept my responsibility and I couldn't live with myself if I gave her away."

"That's all good, but what were you thinking, runnin' off to freakin' Mexico?" Jasmine threw her arms up in the air in frustration.

"Angel, sweetie," Alexis said, her voice a lot calmer than Jasmine's. "What are you doing?"

Angel straightened her back and tried to look defiant. "I'm going to Mexico. What does it look like?"

"It looks like you finally flipped out, that's what it looks like," Jasmine yelled.

"No, I have family on my father's side in Matamoras. I'm going to stay with them." Angel shifted a large black duffel bag on her shoulder.

"Have you talked with your family there?" I asked.

"No, but they'll take me in. I know they will." Angel's eyes filled with tears as she looked away. "They have to."

I knew I had to try and reason with her. I stepped around to face her. "Angel, think about what you're doing. Mexico? What happened to California?"

Angel wiped at her eyes. "I called my aunt there and she told me I couldn't come without my mother's blessings."

"Well, running away isn't the answer," I gently said.

"Then what is?"

I had no idea what to tell her. I just knew Angel needed to find some way to stick around and make it work. "I don't know. Stay in Houston. Get a job. Go to night school. It's not the end of the world. Girls do it all the time."

"You guys just don't understand," Angel said as she tried to step around us. "I gotta go before the bus leaves me."

"Angel, *you* don't understand. Running isn't the answer," I tried to reason.

"Yes, it is," Angel forcefully replied as she turned around. "My mom wants to make me give my baby up."

"So, don't do it," Jasmine said.

"But she can make me."

"She can't make you do anything," Jasmine said, then looked at me. "Can she?"

I shrugged. I wasn't sure, but I knew we at least had to make Angel think no one could take her child. "No, you're old enough now to make that decision yourself."

"It's just hard," Angel said. "I just need to get away. I can't keep being a burden to my sister. I don't have anybody."

"You have us." I slowly walked over and took Angel's hands. "And if you come home, we'll be there for you."

"Yeah, I may not be able to help you out with money, but I can babysit," Jasmine offered. Her tone had softened considerably.

Angel took a deep breath. "I really don't want to go to Mexico."

"Then don't go." I made sure my voice was firm. After seeing Angel, I now knew more than ever that Angel needed to be at home with family and friends.

"Plus," Jasmine added, "do you know what we went through to get here? We almost got killed out in some backwoods."

Angel jerked her head around. "What? What happened?"

I rolled my eyes at Jasmine. "Long story."

"How about we tell you all about it on the way home?" Alexis said.

Angel let out a defeated sigh. "Okay. I only had about thirteen dollars left anyway."

"Thirteen dollars? How were you going to live on that?" It was Alexis's turn to get loud. Angel didn't respond.

"Well, she won't have to worry about that now." I said as I took Angel's hand. "Did you check any luggage?"

"No," Angel responded. "I only have my duffel bag." She patted the big black bag draped over her shoulder.

"You were running away with only thirteen dollars and a duffel bag?" Alexis asked.

Angel shrugged. "I don't know what I was thinking."

"I don't, either," Jasmine mumbled.

After we settled in for the drive back to Houston, I pulled out my cell phone and opened it to see if there were any missed calls. "Shoot!" I muttered.

"What?" Angel asked.

I held up my phone. "Twenty-one missed calls," I said with a groan.

"Twenty-one!" Jasmine exclaimed.

"I'm dead," I said as I dialed in to listen to my messages. My mother had left message after message, each one getting more and more frantic. In the last message she said she was calling the police.

"Dang," Jasmine laughed as she looked at me. "I thought my granny was bad. What, your mother didn't believe you were at Angel's?"

I flipped the phone closed. "Nope, considering Miss Rachel called Angel's mom."

Jasmine laughed harder. "Boy, you are dead. Your mom is going to kill you. I told you you should've listened to me."

I turned around in my seat. "I've also got a message that somebody broke into my car at the church. All my windows are busted out." She looked at Alexis. "Where's your wallet?"

"Huh?" Alexis said. She looked at me like she was trying to figure out what I was talking about. "My wallet?" Alexis kept one hand on the steering wheel as she reached over with her other hand and grabbed her purse. "It's right here," she said as she felt around in her purse. "Oh no," she said, as she dumped everything out. "It's not in here!"

Jasmine leaned up. "You mean we've been on the road with no money!"

"That's not the problem," I said, trying my best to stay calm because I knew we were in a world of trouble. "Alexis's wallet was found in the parking lot of the church. So between my car, your wallet, and us being missing in action, they think something happened to us. My mom, Miss Rachel, Alexis's mom, and even Mrs. Lopez are all at the church waiting on the police to come take a report." I paused. "And, oh yeah, Jasmine, your grandmother and your mother are there, too."

Jasmine stared at me dumbly. "So we're all dead?"

"Exactly," I said as I turned around and leaned back against the seat.

"Guys, I'm so sorry," Angel said. No one responded. I wasn't mad at Angel. I was sure none of us were. After all, I'd gotten in trouble for a lot worse things. Even still, I wasn't looking forward to all the trouble we were in.

Alexis navigated the car back onto the freeway. "Should we call?"

"Probably," I replied.

"Not me," Jasmine said. "I'd rather just wait and take my punishment in person. Besides, maybe they won't kill us outright in front of everyone. If we call, they'll go home and wait. And I want a witness to my murder."

I couldn't help but smile. "You know what, Jasmine? That's the smartest thing I've heard you say all day."

I leaned back and we rode the rest of the way home in silence.

23

Camille

$\mathcal{M}$y head felt like somebody was beating it with a baseball bat. And the person swinging the bat was my mother. She hadn't shut up since I walked in the house. She'd fussed all night long, then woke up fussing again this morning. She'd already put me on punishment, but she continued to torture me by fussing every chance she got. As part of my punishment she took away my cell phone.

I smiled as I patted my pocket for my replacement cell phone. I'd taken the SIM card out of the phone before my mother took it and transferred the card to an old phone, so I was back in business. It was a little trick I'd learned from my friend Melanie, and my mother was none the wiser.

I had been instructed to come straight home today, which I'd done with little complaint. I didn't even complain when my mother made me get up and go look in the mailbox for some check she was waiting on. Right about now, I was glad I checked the mailbox or I might never have known about the letter I was now holding in my hand.

I stared at the legal-size notepaper. Keith's almost perfect handwriting graced all four pages. My gut was telling me to tear it up, to not even read it, anything but give him the satisfaction of getting under my skin.

I was stretched out on my bed, turning the envelope over and over, wondering what it said.

Maybe it was meant for me to see this letter. After all, I never checked the mail. If my mother hadn't been waiting on a payment from the insurance company I wouldn't have checked the mailbox today. And had my mother seen this letter, she would have definitely tossed it out without me ever knowing anything about it.

I paused before throwing the letter in the trash. I was so over Keith and had no interest in anything he had to say. At least, that's what I told myself.

I jumped as my bedroom door flew open.

"Mama, why won't you knock?" I said, clutching my chest.

"In my own house? You've been watching too much TV." She looked around the room. "I thought I told you to clean up this room."

I sighed. *Leave me alone,* I wanted to shout. Instead, I said, "I'm getting to it."

"Get to it now! You know you're in enough trouble as it is, gallivanting all over the country." My mother walked into the room and snatched up an empty Cheetos bag. "And what did I tell you about eating in this room?"

I caught myself before I rolled my eyes. "Mama, I'm sorry. I'll clean up now." I walked over and started picking up my clothes off the floor.

"Camille, first you get arrested, then you go running off out of town, scaring me half to death. Despite all of that, you still won't do what I ask you to do. You know how hard I work. Why must you insist on making things harder on me?"

Oh, here we go with this speech. I knew it by heart

now. I kept my back to my mother as I said the words along with her.

". . . I work my tail off to provide for you and you can't do the little things I ask you to do," I mouthed along. "You take your lifestyle for granted. You want to take. I mean, I can't even get you to get a part-time job to pay for the gas in the car you don't even appreciate."

I turned toward my mother, making sure I was out of striking distance. "It's not like you let me drive the car half the time anyway." There, I'd said it. I'd been wanting to tell my mother how I felt about my car situation for a long time. It was the stupidest thing. I had a car—an old Volkswagon Jetta—but my mother made me ride the bus to school and back. She let me run occasional errands and drive to meetings, but as for everyday use, my mother kept a tight reign on the car.

My mother glared at me. "That's because you have proven time and time again that you are not responsible. And what am I supposed to do? Give you money for gas, because you sure don't have any. I mean, look at you. You left the car in a parking lot and now I have to pay to get the windows fixed. You need to get a part-time job or something, not only for yourself, but to help out around here."

I bit down on my bottom lip. Boy, I wished I could say what was really on my mind. "My daddy said as long as I kept my grades up, I never had to work in school," I said.

"News flash, Camille. Your daddy isn't here!" my mother screamed. She must have realized she was yelling because she covered her eyes and looked like she was trying to calm herself down. She removed her hand and lifted her head. "It's just me, baby. And I need some help from you. I worked when your daddy was here because I wanted to. I work now because I don't have a choice. I miss church because I'm working so much. Do you think I want that?" My mother massaged her temples. "You just don't understand the stress I'm under."

"I miss Daddy, too, Mama," I said when I noticed the look in her eyes.

"Then how can you go take up with some hoodlum just like the one that shot your daddy? Just a slap in the face to his memory."

I sighed. This was another speech I had heard countless times. "Mama, I told you before, Keith didn't have anything to do with Daddy's shooting."

"No, but it was some thug just like him!" My mother began sobbing. "You just make things so much harder on me."

I shook my head. The smallest thing would make my mother break out into tears. It's like, no matter what I did, I couldn't make her happy.

"Mama, I will work harder, okay?" I didn't know if I really would, but at this point I would say anything to keep my mother from crying.

"Fine, Camille." My mother wiped her face. "That's all I ask." She stared at me for a few minutes before turning and walking out of the room.

I continued cleaning up my room while playing out in my mind how much longer I had until my eighteenth birthday. I already had it planned. I was moving on June 4, 2008, the day I turned eighteen.

It only took about twenty minutes for me to clean my room. I picked up the trash can and was headed downstairs to empty it, when my eyes made their way back to Keith's unopened letter.

"No, Camille," I muttered. But it was like something drew me to that letter. *Just open it and read it. What harm is there in that? See what the dog has to say for himself.* I pulled the letter out, then sat the trash can down before plopping down on the bed. I tore the envelope open and began reading.

Dear Camille,

Baby, I really hope you're reading this. When I saw you in court the other day, I didn't expect to feel the way I did. I know you don't believe this but I love you. I didn't get in touch with you sooner because I wanted you to hate me. I thought maybe it would help you get over me faster, but my heart won't let me follow thru with that plan. Camille, you are the best thing that ever happened to me. I just need the chance to explain to you about Shay. It's not like it seems. I don't love her. I don't even want to be with her. I just made a mistake and was trying to man up and take care of my responsibility. Doesn't that count for something in your book? Shay is just a very demanding girl who goes after what she wants—hard. I'm not saying this to make excuses. I'm just saying it because I hope that you will understand that I never wanted to hurt you.

I will say it again. I know I wasn't handling my business like I shoulda been with school and all, but I did not carjack that woman. You know that ain't even me. I think about you every day. I know you're the only one who believed in me and I messed that up. I can't stand it in here, baby, which is why I couldn't take it here anymore. I missed you so much and just wanted to be with you. I have faith in God that I can some way prove I didn't do this. I just hope you will take me back once everybody knows I'm innocent.

I laughed. Take him back? And now he wants to be talking about God. "I ain't never heard him mention God before," I mumbled as I kept reading.

I need to see you to tell you this face to face. Please come visit me during visiting hours next Wednesday. I promise you won't regret it.

Love always, Keith.

I balled the letter up. Keith always did have a way with words. *But what if he's telling the truth? What if he really is innocent?* I couldn't get that little nagging voice out of my head.

No, Keith was a lying dog. He had lied about his girlfriend, lied about being in jail, and had gotten me in a world of trouble. Innocent or not, he was still a lying dog.

I closed my eyes and lay back on my bed as I repeated that over and over again.

24

Camille

The walls seemed to be closing in on me. I looked to my left and saw a woman tearfully kissing the glass. The man on the other side was doing the same. To my right, a couple was arguing because the girl hadn't come to see him last week. Life behind bars.

I shuddered as I tried to peer down the hall and see what was taking so long. I relaxed as much as I could when the door to the room behind my glass opened and Keith poked his head in. He was wearing an orange jumpsuit and flip-flops. His hands and ankles were in handcuffs. He wore his hair back in cornrows. Despite the big cut above his left eye, he was still as cute as ever. I shook myself out of my thoughts and picked up the phone.

Keith sat down and picked up the phone as well. "I didn't think you'd come."

"I shouldn't have," I responded, a hard look across my face. I still couldn't figure out why I was even there. I should have never gotten his letter out of the trash. And I dang sure didn't need to be sneaking off to come here and see him, but I needed to know if he had indeed just been using me. And . . . part of me simply wanted to see him.

I stared through the glass partition. I wanted to reach through and strangle him for the pain he'd caused me. "I'm surprised they're even letting you have visitors." I made sure he knew I had an attitude.

"They weren't. This is the first day I can have them and guess who was the first person I wanted to see?" He flashed a crooked grin that almost made me smile, but I caught myself.

"Is that supposed to mean something to me?"

His smile faded. "No, I just wanted you to know how important you are to me."

I sucked my teeth. "Do I need to get my boots for all the crap you're shooting my way?"

"Dang, girl. Why you so mean?"

"Why do you think, Keith?" I leaned back and tried to calm myself down. "Why did you want to see me?"

"Why haven't you been taking my calls?"

"I'm not accepting any collect calls from you so my mama can kill me. I'm in enough trouble as it is."

Keith tried to move the phone to his other hand, but he dropped it because the handcuffs kept him from moving freely. He muttered a curse word, managed to pick it back up and finally shift it to his other ear. "I hate it in here," he groaned.

"You should of thought about that before you carjacked that woman," I said.

Keith stared at me for a few seconds without saying anything. "So I guess you don't believe me anymore when I say I didn't do it?"

I just glared at him. I wanted to hate him so much, but

that was easier said than done. "I don't know what to believe, Keith." I didn't. I had always believed he didn't do it, but I'd always believed he was faithful to me, too. And I had definitely been wrong about that.

"How long have you been knowing me, Camille?"

"A year."

"And how long were we together before all of this mess went down?"

"Four months, but what does that have to do with anything?"

"I know you didn't like me hanging out with my cousins and stuff. And you didn't like some of the stuff they got into, but you know I never got caught up in all that stuff. At least nothing major anyway." Keith looked like he desperately wanted me to believe him.

"I don't know anything, Keith. Except I almost went to jail fooling with your behind."

Keith sighed. "Look, I asked you here to tell you in person, I'm sorry."

I couldn't take my eyes off of him. Either he was truly sorry or a dang good liar. *Do not let him get to you.* "Sorry about which part? Using me? Lying to me? Or playing me for a fool?"

Keith lowered his head in shame. "All of that. And getting you caught up in this madness."

I hit the window. "I almost went to jail for you, boy."

"I know. I'm sorry. Believe it or not, I love you, girl. And I never wanted to get you caught up in my problems. I just wanted to get out and spend some time with you."

I couldn't help it. He was getting to me. He must've known it because he kept talking, speeding up his words.

"When I broke out, I could've easily gone to Shay's but you were the only thing on my mind," he said.

I cringed at LaShay's name. "Why didn't you tell me you had a girlfriend?"

Keith gave me an apologetic look. "I'm sorry. Shay is . . . special. And I don't mean that in a good way. When I found out she was pregnant, I just, I don't know, just wanted to do right by my child and try and make it work with his mother. I knew she wouldn't let me see my son if I broke it off with her. But Shay is hard to be with. Then I met you at that football game and you were looking all good and stuff. And as I got to know you, you reminded me of the person I was, you know, before I started doing things I didn't have no business doing. I was really feeling you. That's why when I got out, I just wanted to be with you."

I stared at him. He actually looked like he was trying not to cry. "Keith, I was feeling you, too. But you broke out of jail. How long did you think that would last?" I was shocked that the anger that was so strong when I walked into the jail was starting to fade.

Keith shrugged his shoulder. "I don't know. I just couldn't take being in here, especially because I know I didn't do it. When that guard slipped up and left that side door open, I saw my chance and I took it."

"But you hit him. That only made things worse."

"He caught me as I was leaving and I just freaked out," Keith said.

I couldn't believe it. I was actually starting to feel sorry for him. I didn't know what I would do if I was wrongfully put in jail. Maybe I'd break out, too. "Well, look at you now. You've bought yourself more time."

He half-smiled. "You sound like my mama."

I just cut my eyes at him. This was nothing to smile about.

"I know," he continued, "it was stupid. But I just wasn't thinking straight. Can you ever forgive me?" Keith asked, a sincere look across his face.

I thought about it. Not that I enjoyed getting into trouble, but if it wasn't for Keith, I'd have never met Angel, Alexis, and even Jasmine. And I'd found some true friends in them. Besides, Rachel was always talking about forgiveness.

"I'll forgive you, Keith. But that don't mean I'm going to forget what you did," I threatened.

Keith seemed to perk up. "So does that mean I can call you?"

"Ummm, no, it does not." I was not about to let him off the hook that easy. "First of all, I'm not about to be accepting no collect calls. And I don't do baby mama drama. And I can tell already, your baby mama is crazy."

"I guess I have to accept that." He flashed a smile.

"I guess so." I stood to leave. I really needed to get home before my mother made it in from work. Otherwise, I'd have to answer a hundred and one questions about where I'd been. "I hope you get your life together, Keith. Take care." I gently touched the glass before turning to leave.

"Camille?"

"Yeah," I said, turning back around.

"Thank you for coming." He blew me a kiss.

"No problem," I said, ignoring the kiss. "I'll say a prayer for you next time I go to church."

Keith laughed. "Prayer? Yep. Been doing a lot of that since I been in here."

I shot him a smile. "You might not have been in this spot in the first place had you been praying."

Keith laughed again. "Now you sound like my mama *and* my preacher."

I laughed with him as I walked out of the small visiting room. " 'Bye, Keith."

I was still smiling as I made my way back into the jailhouse lobby. My smile faded when I heard the screaming.

"What do you mean he's had his visitor for today? I'm the only one who should be visiting him! Who is it? Who's been here?"

I groaned at the sight of LaShay yelling at the deputy.

"This is some bull! Somebody better open these doors and let me in!" she screamed.

"Ma'am, if you don't calm down, you will be coming in, but it won't be for a visit," the deputy told her. He stood up to face her. "Now, I will say this again. Keith Lee has had his one visitor today. I am not at liberty to tell you who that is, no matter how much you yell. You are more than welcome to come back tomorrow during visiting hours."

"But I have his son." LaShay seemed to be grasping at straws.

"I don't care if you have the Pope. You ain't getting in to see him today." The deputy sat down and began flipping through his magazine.

LaShay huffed before storming off. I hid behind the vending machine in the employee break room, hoping LaShay would just leave. But of course luck wasn't on my side. LaShay plopped down on the bench right by the door.

A sheriff's deputy tapped me on the shoulder. "Ma'am, this is a restricted area. You have to wait in the lobby," he said.

I sighed, then walked out into the lobby with my head held high. I hadn't taken two steps when LaShay saw me.

"You! You're the reason I can't see my man?" LaShay screamed.

Before I could respond, LaShay had left the stroller and her son and come running toward me. She grabbed my hair and threw me to the ground.

"I told you to stay away from him!" She hit me in the eye as she jumped on top of me.

Now, I'm no wimp by any means, but this chick was kicking my butt. She was like a wild woman.

"Get her off of me!" I shouted.

It didn't take long before two deputies grabbed LaShay and pulled her off. She didn't stop swinging or cursing.

A deputy slammed her up against the wall, while another one helped me up off the ground.

"Are you okay?" the female deputy asked me.

I tasted blood. I put my hand to my mouth and cringed. My eye was also killing me and felt like it was swelling up.

"Do you need me to call a paramedic?"

The last thing I wanted was to give LaShay the satisfaction of knowing I had to go to the hospital. "No, I'll be fine."

I watched the deputies drag LaShay into a back room. She was still screaming and cursing. Another deputy got the stroller and pushed it back there as well.

I just wanted to get out of this funky place. I assured the deputy I was fine, told her I didn't want to press charges, and left as fast as I could.

Inside my car, I pulled down my sun visor and surveyed my face in the mirror. I looked horrible. I closed my eyes and tried not to cry. Maybe this was a sign. Maybe God knew Keith was getting to me and wanted to send me a wake-up call.

I started the car and backed up. "I'm awake. I'm definitely awake," I said as I sped out of the jail parking lot.

25

Camille

$\mathcal{I}$ flinched as my mother laid the ice pack against my face. It was just my luck that I pulled up at home the same time my mother did. She had almost died when she saw me bruised and bloody.

Right now, I was sitting at the kitchen table while my mother nursed the bruises on my face.

"Now explain this to me again. You did what?" She didn't give me time to answer. "I can't believe you down there fighting like a common criminal. Lord, have mercy."

"Mama, it wasn't my fault," I cried. I had contemplated telling her that I got jumped at the mall, but as soon as I opened my mouth, I couldn't get the lie out, so I just told the truth. It was a decision I was now starting to regret.

My mother threw the cotton ball she had dipped in alcohol in the trash and turned toward me. "If you wouldn't have had your fast tail down there, you wouldn't have had to worry about getting jumped by anyone."

"But Mama—"

"But my butt. This is ridiculous! Hasn't that boy brought you enough trouble? Not only did you sneak off to see him, but you skipped school to do it and you lied to me about it. You told me you were going to the library!"

I hadn't wanted to lie, but when my mother told me to come straight home from school, I had to come up with a reason because visiting hours didn't start until four. "I didn't skip school, Mama. Just my last class."

"That's skipping school!" My mother paced back and forth across the kitchen. She suddenly swung around and stuck out her hand. "I got the solution for that. Give me your keys."

I was totally confused. "What?"

"I didn't stutter. Give me the keys to your car. I'm going to put the car up until you turn eighteen."

She couldn't possibly be saying what I thought she was saying. The stern expression on her face told me that she was serious. I snatched my purse off the counter, reached inside, grabbed my keys, and slid them toward her. "How am I supposed to get around?"

My mother snatched the keys. "I will take you where you need to go. I told you to stay away from that hoodlum. But since you want to be hardheaded, I got something for you."

"How am I supposed to get to my meeting tonight?"

"I told you, I will take you. Is that group helping anyway?" My mother opened a kitchen drawer and dropped the keys inside. "Obviously not, if you're still sneaking off to see that little thug."

"Yes, it is," I said, as I followed my mother. "You're the one who made me go in the first place. Now that I like it, you act like you don't want me to go."

"Camille, have a seat," my mother said as she turned around.

I plopped down at the kitchen table. I definitely was not in the mood to hear a lecture.

"I know you think I'm hard on you," my mother said as

she sat down across from me. "But you just don't get it. I only want what's best for you. I'm out there busting my behind for you to give you a better life. And when I see you jeopardizing all that I've worked for, all that *you've* worked for, I have a right to be concerned." My mother paused and inhaled deeply. She looked worn out. I felt a twinge of sympathy because I knew I was working her nerves. But I was sixteen years old and it was time for my mother to understand she couldn't dictate my life.

"Mama . . ."

"You know what, Camille?" My mother leaned back in her seat. "I can't deal with you right now. I'm so disappointed in you. Just go to your room."

I thought about arguing but I welcomed getting away from my mother. "Fine." I stomped off to my room. Just as I got there, my cell phone vibrated. I pulled it out of my pocket and looked at the caller ID. Melanie's number popped up.

"Hey, Mel," I said solemnly as I answered the phone.

"What's up with you?" Melanie replied in her usual chipper voice. "Why you sound like that?"

I laid across my bed. "Girl, it's my mom. She is about to drive me nuts."

"Shoot, join the crowd. I'm on punishment as we speak."

"Then what are you doing on the phone?"

"She ain't here, so it doesn't count," Melanie laughed. "What have you been up to? I haven't seen you around much. I was beginning to think you'd kicked me to the curb."

"Naw, I've just been going through some things. You know, dealing with my mom trippin' and getting arrested and all. Then I've been going to those Good Girlz meetings. You know they're making me do that for my community service."

"Oh, I don't mean to cut you off," Melanie interrupted, "but I was just calling to tell you that Eric Jackson asked me out. He said he's been wanting to ask me out since before me and Al broke up."

I tuned Melanie out as she went on and on about the latest boy in her life. My thoughts turned to Alexis, Angel, and even Jasmine. They would listen to my problems. It was sad; Melanie was supposed to be my best friend, but lately I felt a whole lot closer to my new friends.

". . . and then Tonya gon' get all mad because she said she wanted to go with Eric . . ."

I didn't even know what Melanie was talking about. And I was slowly realizing that I didn't really care.

26

Camille

*N*o wonder Alexis thought she was a princess. This room was fit for a queen.

I glanced around Alexis's bedroom, which was the size of three of my bedrooms. Not only did she have a queen-size canopy bed, but she had a sofa, an entertainment center, a desk, a huge dresser, and a vanity table. The room was decorated in a beautiful shade of pink. I would never leave this room if I lived here.

Me and the girls were gathered at Alexis's house watching *American Idol*. Angel was laid out on the sofa. Jasmine was stretched out on the floor eating popcorn. I was on the bed painting my toenails.

"I'm going to try out for the show next season," Alexis said as she got comfortable across her bed.

"What? You're kidding, right? You can't sing," I said as I lifted the nail polish to keep it from spilling when Alexis lay down.

"Yes, I can. Besides, how do you know I can't sing?" Alexis jumped up and grabbed a hairbrush. "I'm a survivor," she sang as she bounced up and down.

"You may look like Beyoncé but you definitely don't

sound like her." Jasmine chuckled as I gave her a high five from across the room.

"Haters," Alexis joked. "Don't ask for any free tickets to my concert when I win and make it big."

"If you ever even get on *American Idol*, I will become your personal servant," Jasmine laughed.

"She just might get on," I added. "You know they put people on just so everybody can laugh at them."

"Whatever." Alexis gave us the hand. "Like I said, you're just a bunch of haters. And you'll be sorry when you see me in Hollywood."

"Like I said," Jasmine repeated. "If you do make it to Hollywood, I'm at your beck and call."

"Did you hear that, Camille? You're my witness," Alexis said. "Angel, you, too." Everyone turned toward Angel, who hadn't moved from the sofa. She had a look of horror on her face.

"Girl, what is wrong with you . . ." I stopped talking as my eyes made their way down to the wet spot on Angel's skirt. "Yuck. Did you pee on yourself?"

"Ewwww," Alexis said as she walked over to the sofa. "I know—"

"My water broke," Angel said, cutting everyone off.

"It's too early, though, huh? You're only eight months, right?" I asked.

Angel nodded, her eyes wide. "I guess my baby is coming early."

"Oh, my God," Alexis said. "You cannot have your baby in my bedroom."

"Alexis, I don't think she'd planned on having her child here. Stop standing there staring and go call for help or something!" I snapped. "Are you in any pain, Angel?"

Angel shook her head but she acted like she was in shock. "Ohmigod, ohmigod."

"Jasmine, grab her arm and try to keep her calm," I ordered.

Jasmine didn't move.

"Jasmine!" I yelled. I didn't really know what I was doing either. But I'd seen enough episodes of *ER* to know that we needed to keep Angel calm until we could get her to the hospital. "Angel, can you walk?"

"I . . . I think so." Angel struggled to stand as Jasmine lifted her by the arm.

"Is her baby going to fall out if she stands up?" Alexis asked.

Me and Jasmine both threw Alexis a crazy look and shook our heads. "That girl is special," Jasmine said.

"No, Alexis," I said as we walked Angel into the hallway. "I don't think the baby can fall out. It's hanging on to the umbilical cord, stupid. Now, can you go see if your mom can take us to the hospital in her SUV? We need to lay Angel down."

"How do you know that?" Alexis asked.

"I don't! I'm just guessing that's what we need to be doing. Now, would you go?"

Alexis turned and scurried out, calling out to her mother as she raced down the hall.

Me and Jasmine helped Angel down the stairs. Angel let out a scream about halfway down.

"Wh-what's wrong?" I asked.

"I just had a sharp pain," Angel cried.

Alexis came racing down the stairs. "My mom isn't in her room." I was the first to notice the arm draped over the side of the couch and the bottle of sleeping pills on the floor next to the sofa. It was empty and lying on its side.

"Can you wake your mom up and ask her to take us?" I asked. I didn't know how out of it she was, but we needed to do something.

Alexis shook her mother. "Mama, wake up."

"Ughhhh," Mrs. Lansing groaned. She didn't open her eyes.

"Angel's about to have her baby and we need your help." Alexis shook her mother harder.

Her mother raised her head. "Huh?" Her hair was matted to her head and her eyes were bloodshot.

"Angel is about to have her baby and we need your help," Alexis repeated.

Alexis's mother squinted her eyes. "You're having a baby?"

"No, Angel is!" Alexis yelled.

"Who's Angel?"

"Angel, my friend, from the church group."

"Ohhhh, yeah." Mrs. Lansing smiled. "You can see angels if you go to church." She dropped her head back on the sofa.

I could tell Alexis was embarrassed.

"Is she okay?" Jasmine asked.

Alexis gently rubbed her mother's hair as she noticed the empty pill bottle. "Yes, she'll be fine. She just takes these pills to help her sleep." Alexis stood up. "She's a little depressed, and the pills help her to sleep."

Alexis took another look at her mother before grabbing her mother's keys off the fireplace mantel. "I'll just use her SUV. She'll understand."

It took twenty minutes to get to the hospital, and that was with Alexis driving like a speed demon. I talked to 911 all the way there and they helped me keep Angel calm. She was now inside a labor and delivery room about to give birth.

"Should we call her mother?" Alexis asked. We were in the waiting room of the maternity ward of Sugar Land Methodist Hospital.

Me and Jasmine looked at each other. "I'm not calling her," Jasmine said.

"Why do I have to be the one to call her?" I protested. I don't know how I became the so-called leader of this group, but they always seemed to turn to me when it came to making decisions.

"You're the most diplomatic," Alexis responded.

Now that was funny. Me, diplomatic?

"Out of all of us, you're the best one to try and reach Angel's mother," Alexis said.

I sighed. We didn't have time to argue over who would call. "You know what? I don't even have her mother's number," I said as I looked at my cell phone address book.

"Call Miss Rachel. She has all of our information. Do you have her number?"

I shook my head. "I haven't had a chance to program anybody's number in."

Alexis handed me her phone. "Her cell number is programmed in my phone."

I took it and scrolled through until I found Rachel's number.

Less than five minutes later, Rachel was on her way and I had Mrs. Lopez on the phone.

"Hola?"

"Mrs. Lopez, you don't really know me," I said. "I'm a friend of Angel's. I met you at your house one day. Angel is, um . . . she's having her baby."

I heard a long pause before the woman said anything.

"Where is she?"

"We're at Sugar Land Methodist. On the floor where they have the babies."

"Okay." Mrs. Lopez slammed the phone down.

I didn't know if that meant she was coming or not. Oh well, I'd done my part. I turned back toward my friends.

"Well, is she coming?" Alexis asked.

"I have no idea," I responded.

"Should one of us go in there with Angel? She's all by herself," Alexis asked, turning her attention to Jasmine.

"Don't look at me. I don't do live births," Jasmine said, plopping down on the hard sofa in the waiting room.

Alexis turned back toward me. "Well, I'm not really good with hollerin' and pain and all that stuff," she said.

I shook my head, wishing Rachel would hurry up and get here. She could handle this stuff. I was just about to say something when a bloodcurdling scream caused me to nearly jump out of my skin.

"Was that Angel?" Alexis asked, her eyes wide.

"I don't know," I said as we all looked down the hall.

"Camille, you have to go in there with her," Alexis pleaded. "Remember, you're the one that told her we'd be there for her."

I suddenly envisioned Angel in tears and alone. "Fine. If they'll even let me in." I walked over to the nurses' station and a few minutes later I gave Alexis and Jasmine the thumbs-up as I headed into Angel's room.

I took a deep breath. When I agreed to be there for Angel, never in a million years did I dream it would be this way.

27

Camille

I was absolutely worn out as I walked into the waiting room and eased down in one of the chairs. I was sweating and I know my hair was all frazzled.

"That was quick," Jasmine said as she stared at me, waiting for a report. "My mama's always telling me how she was in labor with me for one hundred and seventy-two hours."

"Yeah, you were in there less than an hour," Alexis added.

"Well, that's because the baby wasn't waiting," I said.

"What did she have?" Alexis asked.

"A little girl." I smiled brightly. "She's tiny but she's beautiful." I looked up at the door just as Rachel rushed in.

"I'm sorry. I got here as fast as I could. How's Angel?" Rachel said.

"She's fine, resting. They just took the baby in for some testing," I said.

"Where's her mother?" Rachel asked, looking around the room.

Alexis shrugged. "She's not here. We don't even know if she's coming."

Rachel shook her head. "So she went through this alone?"

"Camille was in there with her," Alexis said.

Rachel seemed to relax, and a smile crossed her face. "Camille, that was very mature of you to step up to the plate like that."

"It's not like these busters left me any choice." I stood up and dabbed some of the sweat off of my forehead. "They should make all teenagers witness a birth because I tell you, it would sure curb teenage sex. I mean, after what I just saw, I don't want to have any kids until I'm real old, like thirty-five or something."

Rachel busted out laughing and I was too exhausted to try and figure out what was so funny.

The waiting room door swung open and Mrs. Lopez walked in with a slender, pretty olive-skinned girl by her side. "Hi, I'm Rosario, Angel's sister. This is our mother," the girl said. "Which one of you is Camille?"

I raised my hand. "Hi. Angel was hoping you'd come."

Mrs. Lopez didn't reply. She just stood there clutching her Bible and some beads with what looked like a Christmas ornament on the end of them.

"How is she?" Rosario asked.

"Good. She had a little girl."

"She had the baby?" Rosario said, a look of concern across her face. "We missed the birth?"

"Yeah. The baby came pretty fast," I said.

Mrs. Lopez took a deep breath as her eyes filled with tears. I wasn't sure what she was upset about, but at that point, I didn't really care. My work was done. Angel had dang near torn my arm off, she was screaming and crying so hard. I was too young for this madness. Let Angel's family take it from here. "She's in room 221," I said as I pointed down the hall.

"Thank you." Rosario turned and rushed out of the waiting room. Mrs. Lopez took her time following, like she wasn't sure she really wanted to go.

I watched as Angel's mother finally made her way down the hall.

"So, did you see a bunch of blood and stuff?" Jasmine asked.

I rolled my eyes. "Something is wrong with you."

Jasmine ignored my comment. "So did you see the baby come out?"

"Look, if you wanted a play-by-play, you should have been there," I said.

"Did it hurt her?" Alexis chimed in.

I cocked my head. "What do you think, Alexis? She kept screaming, 'Get it out, get it out.' Then she started talking about being punished, how the pain was her punishment."

"Ewww," Alexis huffed. "I'm adopting. I can't even imagine going through all of that pain."

"When I have kids, I'm just going to have them cut my baby out," Jasmine replied. "My cousin had a C-section done and you don't have to push or nothing. They give you some drugs, knock you out, and when you wake up, bam! You got a baby."

"For real?" Alexis asked.

"Didn't you learn that in sex education?" I asked.

"We don't have sex ed at St. Pius."

"Oh, I forgot. Rich, spoiled kids don't need to know about sex," Jasmine laughed.

Alexis ignored her and turned back to me. "Was it really that bad?"

I nodded. "It was really that bad." I thought back to the excruciating pain Angel had been in and shuddered. Nope. That wouldn't be me. This having babies stuff was for the birds. If I didn't know anything else, I knew that. Especially after what I'd just seen.

28

Camille

I hit my computer, trying to figure out why I was having such a hard time logging on to the Internet. Angel had been released from the hospital yesterday and the hospital had pictures of baby Angelica on their nursery website.

Although I had seen the baby in person, I wanted to pull up a copy of the picture and show my mother.

Finally, after several error messages, the hospital's virtual nursery page popped up. I had just put in Angel's name when my cell phone rang.

I glanced at the phone; the number came up as unknown. "Who is this blocking their number?" I muttered as I pressed the answer button.

"Hello."

"Hey, beautiful. You miss me?"

I sighed. This fool had a lot of nerve. Just because I said I forgave him, what made him think he could call me like nothing was wrong? "What do you want, Keith?" I ignored the fluttering in my stomach.

"You."

"Tell that to your baby mama."

"Camille, don't be like that."

"Be like what, Keith? You know what? Forget it. What

do you want with me? And where are you calling me from anyway, since this call wasn't collect? Don't tell me you broke out of jail again!"

"Calm down, baby. I didn't break out or anything else illegal." He paused. "Didn't I tell you I was innocent and that I was gonna get out of here?"

I was shocked at how confident he sounded. That was always a trait I'd liked about him, but he was in jail so how he was still all cocky was beyond me. "Keith, what are you talking about?"

"I told you I didn't carjack that woman."

I got up from my computer and walked over to my bed. "Keith, stop with the lame lies. You were on videotape," I said as I fell back on the mattress.

"No, that was my half brother, Kirk, on the tape. And they caught him, and he confessed."

Half brother? Did Keith actually think I was stupid enough to fall for that? "Whatever, Keith. Tell that mess to someone else."

"I swear to you. I told you I didn't do it," he said with even more confidence.

"If you say so."

"I'm serious, Camille. I knew who it was, but I couldn't be no snitch."

"So you were just gon' do your stepbrother's time?"

"It would have been his third strike. So I took the fall for him. I thought I could handle it. But I couldn't, which is why I broke out when I had a chance."

I didn't say anything. He wasn't going to make a fool of me again.

"I know you don't believe me," Keith continued. "But watch the news tonight. It's going to be on Channel 26.

They talked to my attorney and everything. I still have to come back to court on the escape charge, but my lawyer says he thinks he can get that dropped too since the first charge was bogus."

I didn't know what to think. He sounded so convincing. I flipped over on my stomach. "So what if you are telling the truth, Keith. That doesn't change the fact that you lied to me about LaShay."

"I told you, I'm sorry."

"And I told you, I'm through."

"Camille, don't do this. I love you."

I froze. Why'd he have to go there? He must've known he was getting to me because he softened his voice. "Watch the news. See that I'm telling the truth, then come meet me. I need to see you. I miss you so much. I want you to give me another chance."

I shook off the longing that was creeping up in my heart. "Whatever, Keith. I don't care if you get out of jail. Tell it to your girlfriend, because I don't want to hear it." I flipped the phone closed before he could say another word. I had to because one more minute on the phone and I would've agreed to anything he wanted.

29

Camille

There had to be fifty kids running around the parking lot of Zion Hill Missionary Baptist Church. The entire parking lot and adjacent field had been transformed into a giant neighborhood fair. There were all kinds of games and tables of people selling everything from food to incense to books.

I hadn't really felt like coming out to work the fair today—I had a lot on my mind—but Rachel wasn't hearing it. This was part of our community service, so here we were, working the balloon and face-painting booths.

A little freckle-faced boy cocked his head to the side and squinted. "It doesn't look like a poodle to me," he said with a frown on his face.

"Here, boy." Jasmine pushed the balloon creation at him. It was a long, blue balloon twisted all different types of ways. "It is a poodle. It's a rare breed found only in the jungles of India."

"For real?" the little boy asked.

"Yep." Jasmine leaned in, looked around, then lowered her voice. "And rumor has it that it has magical powers that you can begin using on your fifth birthday."

"Magical powers?"

Jasmine nodded.

The little boy's eyes got wide. He seemed mesmerized. "Whoa, I turn five next month."

Jasmine stood up and smiled. "Well, don't bust that balloon before then."

The little boy grinned, showing all of his teeth. He took off running, no doubt to go show his friends.

I shook my finger at Jasmine. "Shame on you for lying to that little boy, and on church grounds at that."

"What? What's the big deal? It's called imagination," Jasmine protested.

"It's called lying," I replied.

"Would you two stop yappin' your jaws and finish blowing up those balloons? We have a whole line of kids," Alexis said as she painted a rose on a little girl's face.

"Too bad Angel's missing all the fun," Alexis said.

Angel was at home resting because the baby was wearing her out. Although she tried to act like everything was fine, when I talked to her earlier today, I could hear in her voice that it wasn't.

We spent the next hour painting faces, blowing up balloons, and entertaining kids. I breathed a sigh of relief when one of the organizers gave us the go-ahead to start wrapping things up.

"I am so tired," I said as I waved good-bye to the last child.

Alexis picked up a big box and began loading supplies into it. "You. I can't wait to get home and crash." She looked over at me. "Now that we're done, you want to tell us what is wrong with you? You seem like your mind has been somewhere else all day."

Dang. I thought I had done a good job of acting like nothing was wrong. Obviously, I hadn't. It's just that no matter what I did, I couldn't stop thinking about Keith. "I just . . . nothing, never mind." I shouldn't say anything. Part of me was really excited that me and Keith might work things out. The other part was torn over whether it was even the right thing to do.

"Would you spit it out? What's going on?" Alexis said.

"It's Keith." I picked up a pack of balloons off the ground and dumped them in the box.

Jasmine stopped what she was doing and turned to me. "As in your ex, Keith?"

"Yeah, the one and only. He's coming home," I said, trying not to let my excitement show.

"What!" Alexis and Jasmine shouted together.

"Yep, and he wants to see me." I tried to act like what I was saying was no big deal.

"You told him where he could go, didn't you?" Jasmine asked.

I didn't respond. I just continued stacking stuff in the box.

"I know you're not going to see him." Jasmine walked over and stood in front of me.

"He's innocent."

"Yeah, that's what most jailbirds say," Jasmine said sarcastically.-

Now I was wondering why in the world I had opened my mouth. It seemed like I couldn't talk to anybody about me and Keith.

"Camille, tell us you're not for real." Alexis was trying to be her usual diplomatic self.

I let out a frustrated sigh. "He told me about it and I didn't want to believe it myself. But I saw the news with my own two eyes. They said the real carjacker had been caught and had confessed. It's his half brother. Everybody always said they look alike and I guess the cops just made a mistake. He's already out. So y'all can just get off his back because he's innocent. For real."

Both Alexis and Jasmine stared in disbelief. "Okay, maybe he is innocent. But that doesn't change the fact that you went to jail for him," Alexis said.

"Or the fact that he has a girlfriend and a child," Jasmine added.

"Forget I even said anything." I continued cleaning up the booth, hoping that they'd just let the conversation drop. "It's no big deal."

"It's a big deal if you're even thinking about giving him another chance," Jasmine said.

I was tired. It had been a long day. My mind was racing a million miles a minute. And the last thing I felt like doing was being ganged up on by my girlfriends.

"You know what," I said, staring at both of them. "I should've never said anything. It's not like I'm getting back with him. I just see no need to be ugly to him, that's all. So get over it." I stomped off before they could protest.

30

Camille

I knew I shouldn't be doing what I was doing. I knew I shouldn't be in the car with Keith, let alone listening to anything he had to say. But my heart wouldn't cooperate when I was telling it to get over him. He got out of jail last Monday and called my cell every day until Friday, when I finally took his call.

After that call, we ended up meeting Friday evening. We went to the movies Saturday and spent all day Sunday together. Things were just like they used to be. He picked me up from school today and we'd hung out until it was time for me to go to my meeting. I had to lie to my mother again, but I had such a great time with Keith, it was worth it.

"Pull over right here." I pointed to the convenience store across the street from the church.

"I thought you said your meeting was at the church," Keith said.

"It is. I . . . I just want to walk the rest of the way."

"Camille, that's crazy. It's raining. Let me drop you off in front of the church."

I wanted to protest, but I also really didn't want to be walking in the rain. At the same time, I wasn't ready to let anyone know I was even talking to Keith, let alone giving him another chance.

Keith cut off the car and took my hand. "Camille, are you ashamed of me?"

"It's not that." I paused and looked down.

"Well, what is it, then? Baby, I'm innocent. You knew that all along. You were the only one who believed in me and your love got me through this." He let go of my hand and gently caressed my cheek.

I cut my eyes at him. I could feel us falling back in the groove of things. But part of me was still unsure. "Keith, are you on the up-and-up? Don't play games with me, boy."

"Camille, I could be with any girl I want, and I choose you. Our relationship is nothing to be ashamed of."

Before I could say anything else, Keith started the car back up and pulled up to the church. Jasmine's grandmother was dropping her off just as we pulled up.

"'Bye, baby," Keith said. "You want me to come back and get you?"

"Naw, I'll have Alexis drop me off." I reached for the door.

"Can I have a kiss?"

I looked over at Jasmine, who was standing near the car staring at me. I looked back at Keith, but didn't move.

"Oh, so it's like that? You can't kiss me in front of your girl?"

Man, forget it. My girls would just have to get over it. I leaned in and quickly kissed Keith on the lips. " 'Bye. I'll call you later tonight."

"I'll be waiting." Keith smiled as I stepped out of the car.

"Who was that?" Jasmine asked as I walked toward the church door. I ignored her and kept walking.

"Who was that, Camille? Was that Keith?"

I kicked myself for even telling them that Keith was getting out.

I spun around. "And? So what if it was?"

Jasmine stood with her mouth gaped open. "You've got to be joking. I know you're not back with that fool."

"I will say it again, he's innocent."

"I don't care. He's a dog," Jasmine replied.

I was getting irritated. "Jasmine, look, this isn't any of your business. So I would appreciate it if you would stay out of it."

"Stay out of what?" Alexis asked as she walked up.

Jasmine stood glaring at me. "Your friend here is back with her convict two-timing boyfriend."

"Oh, my God! You're not serious, are you?" Alexis turned to me.

"As a heart attack," Jasmine said.

"I am not back with him," I said defensively. "We're just hanging out." I didn't know why I was lying.

"Camille, I know you're not giving him another chance," Alexis said.

This is exactly why I didn't want people to know me and Keith were back together. I couldn't stand having to explain myself and having people constantly judging me. "Look, are we going to see Angel and the baby after the meeting or what?" I folded my arms and tried to change the subject.

"We're not talking about Angel right now. We're talking about you," Jasmine said.

I threw my hands up. "You know what? I don't have time for a bunch of jealous so-called friends to be all up in my business." I knew I was being a bit harsh, but they were getting on my last nerve and I was sick of people bad-mouthing my man.

"Jealous?" Jasmine laughed. "Of what? A lying, no-good, jailhouse dog?"

I stared angrily at Jasmine. "You don't even know Keith. You're just mad because you wish you had somebody who loves you like Keith loves me."

Jasmine stared at me in disbelief. "Just say no," she said.

"What are you talking about?" I responded.

"Just say no to those drugs you must be taking," Jasmine snarled.

"Whatever, Jasmine." I flicked my hand up at her.

Alexis stepped in front of Jasmine as Jasmine balled up her fists. "Y'all, what are we doing? We're letting some guy come between us?" She turned to me. "She's just worried about you, that's all."

"I don't need nobody to worry about me. I can take care of myself," I snapped.

Alexis tried to reason with me. "But he did get you in so much trouble. You said so yourself. You deserve better than Keith. Why would you give him the chance to play you again?"

I was so sick of defending my relationship. If it wasn't with my mother, it was with them. "Look, neither one of you know enough about my relationship to be trying to give your two cents. Just because we're in this stupid group together and we've been hanging out for a few months doesn't mean you know me and my man."

"Oh, so he *is* your man?" Jasmine said, cutting me off.

I planted my hands on my hips. "So what if he is?" They wanted the truth? I'd give them the truth. "We are back together and ain't nothing you can say about it. This is between me and him and if you don't like it, too bad. It ain't like I need your friendship anyway."

"Oh, really?" Jasmine said.

"Really." I knew I probably shouldn't go there, but I was mad and didn't really care. "It ain't like your ghetto behind is even the type of person I'd hang around with anyway. You need to be worried about finding out who your daddy is instead of worrying about me. And Alexis, you need to go see about your crazy depressed mama and get out of my business." I immediately regretted saying that, but it was too late.

Jasmine stood there with her mouth open. She stared at me before spinning and stomping off.

Alexis looked at me with tears in her eyes. "That was foul, Camille."

I didn't respond. I didn't know what to say.

"I hope you and your man are very happy." Alexis turned and took off after Jasmine.

I was still standing outside under the church awning a few minutes later when Rachel stepped out.

"Hey, Camille. I was wondering where you all were." Rachel looked around the parking lot. "Where is everybody? It's after six."

I took a deep breath to keep from crying. "Miss Rachel, have I completed the terms of my community service?"

Rachel looked confused. "Yes, Camille, you know you have. But I thought you wanted to keep coming because you really enjoyed the group." Rachel looked out across the parking lot again. "Is that Alexis driving off?"

I nodded.

"You want to tell me what's going on?"

"I've changed my mind," I said. "Thank you for allowing me to take part in the Good Girlz. I won't be back." I snapped my umbrella open, turned, and walked off down the street to go call Keith to come back and get me. I ignored both the rain pouring down around me and Rachel's calls for me to come back.

31

Angel

I grabbed a pillow and put it over my head. I had been out of the hospital for two weeks and it seemed as if the baby had been crying nonstop every day. I had looked online, browsed baby books, everything under the sun to try and figure out what I was doing wrong. But nothing was working. Angelica wouldn't stop hollering and it was driving me insane.

"Will you shut that kid up?"

I looked up from my spot on the sofa and rolled my eyes at Larry, my sister's boyfriend. His big, hairy belly hung over his boxer shorts. His long hair sat wildly on top of his head like a mop. He looked like a big bear that had just come out of hibernation.

"It's bad enough I have to deal with all these other brats fighting all day, now I have to deal with a screaming baby!" Larry said.

I wanted to tell him to go jump off a building or something. It wasn't like he had a job to go to tomorrow morning anyway. At this point I wished I had gone home with my mother. But when she walked into the hospital room talking about the Hartfords and how they would love the baby, I knew there was nothing to say to her.

I groaned as I pulled myself up off the sofa. I couldn't for the life of me understand why Rosario kept Larry around. He didn't work, didn't help out around the house, and was always talking about her kids. But I didn't need the drama so I reached into the bassinet and picked Angelica up.

"Shhhhh, it's gonna be all right," I whispered as I bounced the baby up and down. Right about now I wished my mother were here to help me figure out what to do.

Angelica continued to yell at the top of her lungs.

"This is ridiculous!" Larry screamed. "It's three o'clock in the morning. That brat is gonna wake up the whole neighborhood. The neighbors are already complaining about all the crying and noise she's been making every night."

I walked back and forth across the living room, trying to soothe Angelica back to sleep. "Please, please, baby. Go to sleep. Stop crying." I gently rubbed the back of Angelica's head. One of the books said babies found that soothing. It wasn't working for Angelica.

I was just about to scream myself when I looked up to see my groggy sister standing in the doorway.

"What's going on?" Rosario asked.

"What's been going on every night for the last two weeks?" Larry barked. "That stupid baby won't stop crying."

"Larry, don't call the baby stupid," Rosario said as she rubbed her eyes and walked into the living room.

Larry ran his fingers through his hair. "Look, Rosario, this is too much. I can't deal with all of this noise."

"Well, what do you want me to do, Larry? That's my sister and my niece. I can't just throw them out."

Angelica's screams seemed to get louder. Rosario turned to me. "What's wrong with her?"

I was on the verge of tears myself now. "I don't know." I bounced the baby harder.

"Stop bouncing her like that." Rosario walked over and took the baby from me and tried to rock her soothingly. "Don't you know you don't bounce her up and down like that?"

"How am I supposed to know that?" I sighed.

Rosario felt Angelica's bottom. "She's soaking wet. When's the last time you changed her diaper?"

I plopped down on the sofa and covered my face. When was the last time I'd changed her diaper? I couldn't remember. I'd spent all day in the house, feeding the baby, cleaning the baby, taking care of the baby. I'd slept in spurts and felt delirious. Camille and the crew were supposed to come by earlier but I couldn't even muster up the strength to call and find out why they didn't show.

"Where are her diapers?" Rosario asked.

I leaned over and grabbed the diaper bag off the floor. I opened the bag up only to find there were no more diapers. "Oh no. I'm out."

"You're what?" Rosario said, raising her voice. The outburst startled Angelica, who had begun to calm down some. She started wailing again.

"I . . . I don't have any."

"How could you not have any diapers?" Rosario asked.

"The ones the hospital gave me are gone. I . . . didn't have any money to get more," I said as I lowered my head in shame. What kind of mother was I?

"Angel! And you know I don't get paid until Friday. I'm flat broke. What are you going to do?"

They both turned their heads to Larry, who was standing in the doorway.

"Don't look at me. I ain't got no money and if I did I wouldn't be spending it on no diapers," he said with a grunt.

I could no longer hold it in. My chest felt like it was getting tight. I tried to talk but found myself only able to take short breaths. "Ro . . ." I grabbed the side of the sofa. "I . . . can't . . . breathe."

Rosario immediately laid the baby down, dug in my purse, and pulled out an inhaler. She put it to my face. "Breathe, Angel. Calm down and breathe," she said gently.

It took a minute of inhaling, but I felt my breathing return to normal. Rosario moved the inhaler. "You okay?"

I nodded.

"Good grief," Larry said. "She has asthma?"

Rosario wiped my forehead. "Yes, but it doesn't flare up often. Are you sure you're okay?" she asked me again.

"I'm sure."

Rosario turned her attention back to Angelica, who was screaming so hard she was starting to turn red. Rosario sighed. "Larry, go get me one of those towels on the second shelf out of the hall closet." She adjusted the baby on the sofa before taking off the dirty diaper. She wiped Angelica down just as Larry returned and handed her a medium-size towel. Rosario folded the towel in half then placed it under the baby. She grabbed two safety pins from the diaper bag and pinned both sides of the makeshift diaper over the baby. Angelica's cries calmed down a little as she started to desperately suck her fingers.

"I guess you haven't fed her, either?" Rosario asked. I just stared at her in a daze.

"She probably doesn't have any food for her." Larry smirked.

I shook my head, trying to come out of the trance I seemed to be in. "Sh . . . She has a bottle on the counter."

"On the counter?" Rosario said as she handed Angelica to me. "Good grief, Angel. You can't leave her bottle out. The milk will go bad and you can't afford to be wasting milk." Rosario raced into the kitchen. I sat holding the baby, who alternated between sucking her fingers and crying. Rosario returned with the bottle. "The milk has soured, Angel." She slipped on her house shoes. "Let me go next door and see if Lupe has any formula. She has grandkids." Rosario left the apartment muttering something I couldn't make out.

Larry stood in the doorway shaking his head. "You are pathetic," he said as he turned and walked back into the bedroom.

I wished I could die right then and there. Larry was right. Not only could I not afford this baby, I didn't know what to do with her anyway. I felt tears start again. I wasn't physically, emotionally, or financially ready to have a child. The sooner I accepted that, the better off everyone would be.

32

Angel

I could do this. I had to keep telling myself that, or else, I would turn and bolt down the street.

I was standing on my mother's porch. I had wrestled with my decision all day long. My eyes were puffy from all the crying I'd been doing. But I knew I didn't have a choice. I wasn't ready to be a mother. I *couldn't* be a mother.

I had been stressed out all day long. I would cry one minute and go off on somebody the next. I'd even hung up on Camille when she'd called trying to tell me some drama about Alexis and Jasmine. I planned to call Camille later and apologize. It's just that right now, I had a whole lot on my mind.

I glanced down at Angelica, who was snuggled in a baby carrier against my chest. Rosario had returned with diapers and formula, and after Angelica was changed and full, she finally drifted off to sleep. I spent the next hour staring at my baby. She was the most beautiful thing I'd ever seen. Right now, she was sucking on her pacifier while she slept. I couldn't help but smile as I caressed her face.

"I hope you can forgive me for this. It's for the best. You deserve so much better." I wiped away my tears before ringing the doorbell. I waited a few minutes and was about to ring it again when the door swung open.

"You came home," my mother said as she looked at my bag, which was sitting at my feet. She looked up at me, relief across her face.

"I hope it's okay." I hesitated. "I need help."

Although Rosario hadn't put me out, Larry had threatened to leave if he had to spend one more night with that "hollerin' baby." Like it or not, my sister loved that man and would be sick if he left, so I left instead.

"It's not easy, is it, *mija?*"

I shook my head as I prepared for a lecture.

"And it doesn't get any easier," my mother warned. "You have no idea what you're in for. You have no money, no place to lay your head, no way to feed your baby. You will live off welfare and struggle, and I never wanted that for you. Do you know how humiliated I was when I had to go on welfare to feed my children? But it was the only way I could survive. I try—"

I had prepared myself for all of this, but standing here listening to it was making me sick. "I'll do it." I cut my mother off.

"Excuse me?"

"I said, I'll do it. I'll give her up for adoption," I said softly. "I came to see if you think . . ." I took a deep breath. These had to be the hardest words that ever came out of my mouth. "If you think the Hartfords still want to adopt my baby."

My mother stared at me, probably trying to see if I was serious.

"I can't do this," I said when my mother didn't respond. "I know now that Angelica would be better off with the

Hartfords, someone who can give her a better life." I rubbed my baby's back. "They'll never love her as much as me, but they can give her so much more than I can. They can take care of her better than I can. She deserves better than what I can give her." I was trying not to break down in tears.

My mother stood silent for a few seconds. "I told you it was not easy. This is not house you're playing," she said.

"Is it too late for the adoption?" Couldn't my mother see this was hard enough as it was?

My mother stepped aside and motioned for me to come in. "I'm sure it isn't. They were desperately seeking a child. God has not blessed them with one. And that baby . . ." She pointed to her granddaughter. "That baby can be God's blessing to them. Out of the bad shall come good," my mother declared. "As long as you trust in Him you will be forgiven. This isn't easy for me, either. But I've prayed for guidance and I think this is the answer. This is a way to atone for your sins, by giving the Hartfords that child. It is a sacrifice for your sins." My mother smiled. "Come, put the baby to rest. I will make the call first thing in the morning."

I unhooked the baby carrier and removed Angelica. My heart ached as I walked into my old bedroom and laid the baby on my bed. I stared at her for several minutes before flipping the light off and walking back into the living room.

"Do you want me to fix you something to eat?" my mother asked.

I nodded. I would love to have a home-cooked meal.

My mother started humming as she made her way into the kitchen. She stopped just before she reached the kitchen entrance. She walked back over and stared at me. "*Mija*, this is for the best. I promise you it is."

I numbly stared at her before breaking down in a huge sob. My mother took me in her arms and held me tightly. "You don't understand right now, but one day you will. You will," she said as she rocked back and forth. With the pain I felt in my heart right now, I just didn't see how that would ever be possible.

33

Camille

It had been a long time since I felt as good as I was feeling right now. I looked at my behind in the full-length mirror, trying to make sure the jeans showed off all the right curves.

"You do look cute," I told my reflection. My smile faded as I thought about Alexis and Jasmine, both of whom had turned their backs on me. Just because I wouldn't let them run my life. And Angel was too caught up in her own drama. When I tried to call and tell her what was going on, she blew me off. That made me mad and I all but wrote Angel off, too.

"Forget all of them," I mumbled as I took the jeans off. "I don't need them when I have my baby." I blew a kiss to Keith's picture, which I had dug out of the drawer I had thrown it in.

I pulled my journal from under my mattress and opened it to an empty page. I loved writing my feelings down and couldn't help but be excited as I lay across my bed and wrote about me and Keith getting back together.

I finished my entry and smiled as I closed the journal. I was on cloud nine as I thought of the special evening Keith had planned. He wouldn't tell me what it was, only that I was in for the surprise of my life.

All the haters would just have to get over it. Me and Keith were meant to be together. People just didn't understand that our love was real. I knew in my heart he was sorry for not telling me about the baby or LaShay.

I sat my journal on the nightstand and got up to take a shower. I turned up the volume on the Missy Elliot song that was blaring from the stereo system in my room so that I could hear it over the running water.

Yep, life was good. Me and my boo were back together and things couldn't be better. I stepped in the shower and began lathering up. I sang along with Missy while I smoothed Pear Glaze body wash all over my body.

Fifteen minutes later I was out of the shower and drying myself off. I grabbed my robe, draped it over my body, then made my way back into my bedroom.

I almost fell out on the spot when I saw my mother sitting on the edge of my bed. She had my journal clutched in her hands and she had a stunned look on her face.

"You read my stuff?" I asked, rushing into the room. I reached out to snatch the journal out of her hands but her glare stopped me in my tracks.

"Don't even think about snatching this from me," my mother growled as she slowly stood up.

I stepped back. "I . . . I just can't believe you read my journal." Why did I leave that thing out? I wanted to kick myself.

"I didn't read the whole thing. Just this page," she said as she held up the book. "The one you wrote today about you and your thug boyfriend."

"I can't believe you read my stuff. That's private."

"When you start paying some bills around here, then you can have some privacy. Until then, anything in my house I will read, take, or anything else I feel like doing. Now, do you want to explain this?" She shook the journal.

"Not really," I mumbled.

My mother's nostrils flared. I just knew I was about to get my two front teeth knocked out.

"Camille Simone Harris. I do not have the time nor the energy to deal with your smart mouth," my mother growled as she stepped toward me. "Now, I'm going to ask you again before I commence to beating you upside your head. What is this about?" She continued to wave the journal in the air.

I walked around my mother and sat down at my small vanity table. "You read it. Me and Keith are back together," I said like it was no big deal. Inside, I was kicking myself for ever even writing down my personal thoughts.

My mother inhaled deeply as she closed her eyes. "Lord, I know this child did not just say what I thought she said."

"What's wrong with us getting back together, Mama? You know he didn't carjack that woman. You saw the news. I told you he was innocent from the beginning." I began brushing my hair, silently wishing my mother would go away.

"I don't care what you told me. *I* told *you* to stay away from him. That boy broke out of jail; whether he was supposed to be there or not in the first place remains to be seen. But the bottom line remains that he broke out, went on the run, and left you to take the fall. And not only does he have a girlfriend, he has a child. Camille! What is your problem?" My mother raised her voice, obviously getting more upset.

"Stop yelling at me!" I screamed as I jumped up from the vanity table. I knew I was crossing the line but my mother was making me sick. "You just don't understand. Nobody understands. He loves me! And we're going to be together and there's nothing you or anyone else can do or say about it!" I snatched my clothes off the bed, quickly put them on, then stomped over to my closet. I reached in and grabbed my duffel bag.

"I'll just leave and go stay with Keith. I'm not listening to this anymore," I said as I stuffed clothes into my bag. I half-expected my mother to tackle me to the ground at any moment, but I just didn't care anymore.

My mother looked like she was about to explode. But instead of going off like I thought she would do, she walked over, grabbed the clothes in the bag and started pulling them out.

"You big and bad, now, are you? Well, last time I checked, my money bought all these clothes. So if you're leaving, you leave like you came in this world—butt naked!"

I stared at my mother. She couldn't be for real. But judging by the way her chest was heaving up and down, she was dead serious.

"Fine," I said. "Keith will buy me some more clothes." I grabbed my purse and car keys off the dresser and started toward the door.

My mother jumped in front of the bedroom door. "Awww, naw, Miss Thang." She held out her hand. "That's my car, so hand over the keys."

"What! Daddy gave me that car."

"No, *me* and your daddy gave you that car. And if you look at the paperwork, you won't find your name anywhere on it. And if you walk out of this house with my car, I will call the cops."

I didn't think I'd ever seen my mother this mad. "I don't believe you would do that."

"Try me."

I weighed my options. I was amazed that my mother hadn't beat me senseless by now, but I wasn't backing down, either.

"Let Keith buy you a car, too," my mother said as she kept her hand out.

I wanted to slam the car keys into my mother's palm, but I knew that might definitely send her over the edge. I bit my lip as I slowly dropped the keys in her hand.

"And I do believe I bought those Orange Bottom jeans you have on."

I cut my eyes. "It's Apple Bottoms."

"I don't care if it's apples, oranges, or tomatoes. They're mine. Take them off."

"You expect me to go out with no pants?"

"You're the one all big and bad. Didn't you buy some warm-ups with that money you got for your birthday? Put them on, because you're not walking out of here with anything my money bought."

At that very moment, I wished I was brave enough to curse my mother out. But since I didn't have a death wish, I kept my thoughts to myself.

"Why are you doing this?" I cried as I started unbuttoning my pants.

"Everything I do, I do in your best interest." My mother kept her firm expression.

"Why can't you understand that we love each other?"

"Love? You're sixteen years old. You don't know what love is. I can tell you what it *ain't*. It ain't some two-bit lying hoodlum, fugitive." My mother clutched her chest and took a deep breath. "All this drama is making my heart hurt." She grabbed a hold of the wall to steady herself. "Lord, I don't know where I went wrong with you." She shook her head and waved me away.

I hesitated. My mother looked like she was having a hard time catching her breath. "Mama . . ." I paused when I noticed she had started crying.

"Keep the jeans. Just go. Just get out of my house if you're going." My mother started rubbing her chest.

"But—"

"Go! Just go! I'm tired. I'm so tired." My mother leaned against the wall. Even though she had her eyes squeezed shut, tears were still trickling down her cheeks.

I was stunned and didn't know what to say. Part of me wanted to go hug my mother, but the other part knew I had to let her see I was serious. Keith was my future and, like it or not, my mother was just going to have to accept that.

" 'Bye, Mama," I said as I walked out of my bedroom, down the stairs, and out the front door.

34

Camille

$\mathcal{I}$ leaned my head back against the passenger seat. I'd called Keith and within fifteen minutes he had come and picked me up at the corner store near my house. We were now riding in his car—or rather, his cousin's car, which he'd been driving since he got out. I had no idea where we were headed. I was just grateful to be away from my mother.

Keith reached over and gently rubbed my hand.

"You gon' be okay?" he asked.

I nodded.

"I still can't believe she just let you leave. Your mother seems like the type that would've beaten your butt, then locked you in your room," Keith laughed.

"Yeah, that's what I thought, too. And she used to be. But ever since Daddy died, she seems to have lost her fight. She just seems tired all the time and all she ever does is cry and give me a hard time." I stared out the window.

"I still can't believe you walked out." Keith shook his head.

I couldn't get the image of my worn-out looking mother out of my head. "I didn't have a choice. As long as I stayed there she wasn't going to let me see you. And now that we're back together, I couldn't have that."

Keith played with my hair. "So you did all of this for me?"

I turned toward him and smiled. "Basically."

Keith smiled back at me. "You know I love you, girl."

"I love you, too."

We rode in silence for a few more minutes before Keith finally spoke. "So, where you want me to take you?"

I sat forward in shock. "Huh? I . . . I just thought . . . well, I assumed I was going to your place."

Keith looked at me like I was crazy. "Why would you assume that?"

"I don't know, we had a date tonight."

"Yeah, but that wasn't until later. I was going to have to take a rain check on that anyway because something came up."

"What?" I couldn't believe him. There shouldn't be anything more important than being with me right now. "Why can't I stay with you?"

Keith pulled his arm back and placed both hands on the steering wheel. He had a look on his face like I was getting on his nerves. "Camille, you know I'm living with my cousin. We're in a one-bedroom apartment and he's barely letting me stay. He's not going to let me bring some chick up in there."

No he didn't. "Some chick?" I snapped.

"You know what I mean. What about your grand-mother's place?"

"That's out. After the last time we went there, my mom took the key and I haven't been back over there since."

Keith had a look of concern across his face. "Well, I

need to drop you somewhere 'cause I got some stuff to take care of."

"Why can't I go with you?" I couldn't believe I had become some whining, sniveling girl, begging to go with her man. I caught myself quickly. "You know what, don't sweat it. Just drop me off at the church."

"Church?"

"Yeah, Zion Hill, where we have the Good Girlz meetings." I crossed my arms over my chest. I was irritated and just ready to get out of the car.

"I thought you left them alone."

"I did. But I'm still cool with Miss Rachel and I need to talk to her about some things." I didn't even know if Rachel was at the church, but I definitely didn't want Keith to think I was sweating him.

"Cool. We can hook up tomorrow or something after you get out of school," he said.

"Whatever," I said as he took off toward the church. I weighed my options. I could call Alexis, but after the way I'd acted with her, I didn't even know if Alexis would take my call. Melanie was out because we hardly talked anymore. I could call my other friend, Tonya, but Tonya's mother was just as crazy as mine and she'd ask a million questions. No, Rachel was my only hope.

We didn't say much as Keith made his way to the church. I was lost in thought and Keith was so busy listening to the radio, he didn't even notice that I was upset. Either that or he just chose to ignore me.

Keith finally looked at me as he pulled into the parking lot. "You gon' be mad at me all day?"

I rolled my eyes but didn't respond. He slowed down

as he neared the front of the church. I opened the door to get out.

"You ain't gon' give me a kiss before you leave?" he asked playfully.

I wanted to go off. He hadn't even asked me where I was going after I left the church or how I was getting there. Then he wanted to sit there and act like nothing was wrong. He knew I'd fallen out with the girls from the group so where did he think I was going?

He pinched my chin and said, "It's gon' be okay, boo. I love you."

I leaned in and gave Keith a quick kiss on the lips.

"See you later, doll," he said with a smile.

I watched as he sped out the parking lot. That fool didn't even stick around to make sure I got in the church safely.

I looked around for Rachel's car. I didn't see it and felt myself fighting back tears. I walked inside the church and asked the secretary when Rachel was expected. After finding out she was due back in about an hour, I sat down outside to wait.

I checked out the massive cross sitting on the lawn of the church and wondered if God was mad at me right now. I didn't mean to disrespect my mother, but I couldn't take it anymore. Hopefully, God understood that.

I didn't realize how long I'd been sitting outside until I saw Rachel pull up into the First Lady spot.

"Camille?" Rachel said as she got out of her Mercedes-Benz.

"Hi, Miss Rachel." I walked over and hugged her.

"It's good to see you," Rachel said. "We missed you at the last few meetings. The girls told me what happened. I was hoping you'd at least call so we could talk."

"I know. I've just been, I don't . . . I've just been busy," I stammered.

"I heard," Rachel responded. I just knew she was about to light into me, too, until I saw the smile on her face.

"So, you don't have anything to say?" I asked suspiciously.

"Please. I'm definitely not one to be judging someone else's decision. I told you—if you knew some of the things I did behind a man . . . " Rachel laughed as she let her words drop. "Where are you headed?"

I shrugged. "I was just kind of waiting on you. My mom and I had it out and I left."

"Left? So where were you headed?"

I didn't respond.

"Tell you what. Why don't you come back to my house and we can sit up and talk. Then tomorrow, you can call your mom and work all of this out," Rachel said.

I wanted to tell Rachel that there was no working anything out. I didn't have anything to say to my mom. But at the same time, I didn't have anywhere else to go.

Rachel must have sensed my hesitation. "Come on, just sleep on it. Run inside with me while I make a few phone calls, then we can be on our way."

I thought about my choices. Keith had already made it clear that he had something else to do tonight.

"You got yourself a deal," I said as I followed Rachel inside the church.

35

Camille

$\mathcal{I}$ was finally starting to feel better. We were in Rachel's car on our way back to her place.

"Ohhh, I love this song." Rachel turned up the volume on the Yolanda Adams song playing on Majic 102.

"I can't believe you listen to that station," I joked. "What would the people at Zion Hill say?"

"Child, you know I don't care nothing about what folks are saying about me, especially those that try to judge me. That's what's wrong with some of these saved folks, always trying to judge somebody." Rachel winked.

"But you're a preacher's wife. I didn't think you were supposed to listen to anything but gospel stations."

"Please. I can love the Lord and R&B," Rachel laughed. "And this is a gospel song anyway. Besides, you know by now I'm not your typical preacher's wife."

"That's for sure," I said with a smile.

Rachel flashed a bright smile back at me just as her cell phone rang.

I reached over and turned down the volume on the radio as Rachel answered the phone.

"Hello," Rachel sang. The smile left her face and she grew quiet.

"Alexis, calm down. Tell me again." Rachel pulled off to the side of the road so she could give her full attention to the phone conversation.

I stared at Rachel. The worried look across her face was scaring me.

"Uh-huh," Rachel said. "How is she? No. Camille is with me."

Now my heart was beating a mile a minute. Why did Alexis want to know where I was?

"Did something happen to one of the girls?" I whispered.

Rachel held up a finger. "Okay, Alexis, you just stay calm. We're on our way."

Rachel pushed the end button on her cell phone.

"What's going on?" I asked.

Rachel slowly turned to me. "It's your mother. She had a heart attack."

I stared at Rachel in disbelief. This had to be a cruel, cruel joke. "What? When, where?"

"Apparently, Alexis went by your house to try and talk to you and she found your mother on the floor. She saw her through the window. She had to call the paramedics to come break in."

"Oh, my God. Is she dead?" My voice began to crack.

"No, but she's in critical condition." Rachel pulled the car back out into the street. "I'll take you to the hospital."

I couldn't keep the tears from coming. Why did I leave? I knew my mother hadn't been feeling well. I knew she was all stressed out and stuff and I still just up and left. This was probably all my fault.

"If she dies, I'll never forgive myself," I whispered.

Rachel reached over and squeezed my hand. "Don't think

like that. Think positive. And pray; that's all we can do."

I closed my eyes. Would God even listen to me with the way I'd been acting lately? I knew all I could do was give it a shot. I hoped God was as forgiving as Miss Rachel always claimed He was because I needed Him now more than ever.

I closed my eyes and said a silent prayer.

36

Camille

It seemed like we'd been waiting for hours. I paced across the waiting room floor for what seemed like the thousandth time.

"Camille, sweetie, sit down and try to relax," Rachel said.

"This is all my fault," I cried. The doctor had given me very few answers, only saying it was "touch and go."

"Stop saying that. This isn't your fault," Rachel replied.

I looked around the waiting room. With the exception of some teary-eyed man who sat in the corner, me and Rachel were the only other people in the waiting room. Alexis was gone by the time we arrived at the hospital. I couldn't really blame her for not sticking around. After all, I had made it clear that I no longer needed nor wanted her friendship. But right about now, what I wouldn't give to have her or Jasmine or Alexis here with me.

I shook off thoughts of my ex-friends and turned my mind to the reason they were ex in the first place. Keith. I needed him here with me.

I walked over toward the window so I could get reception on my cell phone. I punched in Keith's number. After four rings his voice mail picked up. I left a tear-filled message telling him where I was. I knew he'd come running as soon as he got the message.

I had just hung up when the doctor came out. I rushed over to him. "Is my mother going to be all right?"

"Are you Camille?"

"Yes. Please tell me she's going to be fine."

The doctor pushed his glasses up on his nose. He took his time getting his words out.

"It's not looking good right now—your mother has slipped into a coma. We're doing everything we can."

My heart dropped. Rachel put her arms around me. "Can I see her?" I asked.

"I'm afraid not right now. She's being prepped for emergency surgery." The doctor looked down at his chart. "Your mother had a heart attack. It was a mild attack, but we don't know how long she was out before your friend found her." He looked up at me and continued. "We're worried that she may have been deprived of oxygen. But we're really doing everything we can." The doctor tried to flash a reassuring look before he turned and walked out of the room.

I slowly sat down while the shock continued to register. Had my mother's heart problems come from everything I was heaping onto her plate?

Rachel didn't say anything as she pulled me close to her. "It's going to be okay. I've been praying. She'll pull through this. Is there anyone you want me to call?"

I shook my head. "It was just us. My grandmother is in a nursing home and there's nobody else. Mama has a sister in Kansas City but we don't talk to her. I wouldn't even know how to get in touch with her." I began sobbing. I had never felt so alone.

After a few minutes, I pulled myself from Rachel's embrace. "I need to call my boyfriend again."

Rachel nodded and squeezed my hand as I walked back over to the window to use my phone.

"Keith, it's me again," I said after I got his voice mail again. "I really need you. My mother had a heart attack. They don't know if she's going to make it. I'm at Hermann Hospital. Please come."

I had just hung up the phone when I looked up to see Alexis, Angel, and Jasmine standing next to Rachel. I walked back over to where they were standing.

"I hope it's okay that we came," Angel said softly.

I just stared at all three of them. I couldn't believe that they'd come, and I lowered my eyes in shame. "It's more than okay. Thank you for being here."

Alexis and Angel hugged me. Jasmine stayed to the back with her arms folded across her chest. I wanted to hug Jasmine, too, but I knew she would need a little more time to come around. But the simple fact that she was even here meant a lot.

"I'm sorry I wasn't here when you got here," Alexis said. "But I had to go get Jasmine and Angel."

"I'm so glad you're here," I said.

"Where's your boyfriend?" Jasmine snapped.

"Jasmine, don't start," Alexis said.

"I was just asking, that's all," Jasmine said nonchalantly.

I was just grateful to have them there and didn't want to get into it with any of them. "He'll be by later," I replied, still hopeful that he would get my message.

"Umpph, I'll bet," Jasmine said.

Rachel stepped in. "Ladies, I'm going down to the coffee shop. Would anyone like anything?"

All four of us shook our heads.

"Okay, I'll be back shortly. And girls, remember, this is a hospital. No yelling, fighting, or arguing."

"Of course not," Jasmine said with her best fake smile. "We'll be on our best behavior."

Rachel shot her a warning look before making her way out.

I sat down on the waiting room sofa and filled everyone in on the latest with my mother. Everybody looked really concerned, even Jasmine.

"Is that your phone ringing?" Angel asked.

I looked down at my flashing phone, which was clipped to the side of my purse. I picked it up and looked at the caller ID. It was a number I didn't recognize but I answered it anyway.

"Hey, boo."

"Keith?" I could barely hear him and walked over to the window to get better reception. "Where are you?" I asked as I tried to ignore Jasmine's nasty look.

"Uh, I'm a little tied up. I got your message. How's your mom?"

"Keith, they don't think she's going to make it," I cried. "I'm so scared. I need you."

"Well, ah, look here." Keith lowered his voice to a whisper. I could barely make out what he was saying. "I'm not going to be able to . . . ummm . . . get away. I, uh, I'll hook up with you tomorrow."

I walked outside the waiting room because I didn't want everyone all up in my business.

"Keith, did you hear me? My mother could be dying. You can't put whatever you're doing on hold and come be with me?" I didn't care if I had to beg, I needed him right now.

"Naw, skank! He can't come be with you because he's with me!" I was unprepared for the female's voice that came blaring through the phone.

"LaShay, hang up the phone!" Keith screamed.

"I ain't hanging up nothing!" LaShay shouted. "I thought you said you weren't messing with her no more, huh? You lying dog! You hear that, Camille? Keith is a d-o-double-g. You gon' lay up with me all day, then sneak off and call this tramp! Some birthday present, Keith! This is supposed to be my birthday! You make me all these promises about how you gon' do right. How you wanna make it work. How much you love me. You give me this funky tennis bracelet, make me think you serious!"

I was absolutely speechless. He couldn't possibly be doing this to me again.

"What? You ain't got nothing to say now do you, tramp?" LaShay screamed. "I told you to stay away from my man."

"Keith . . . how . . . could you? You're with LaShay? You told me she didn't mean anything," I cried. "You told me you weren't with her."

"Well, he lied. He lives here. Been living here since he got out. And he claimed you ain't nothing but a girl who's stalking him." LaShay seemed to be taking pride in every word.

"Keith, I . . . trusted you . . . I threw away everybody for you . . ." I couldn't even get my words out.

"Camille, wait, let me explain," Keith said.

"Explain it, fool!" LaShay yelled. "Explain how you living with me, over here playing house, talking about getting married and stuff. Even talking to my dang daddy about marrying me. Explain how you using my car, my body—"

I slammed my phone closed. I couldn't take anymore. First my mother. Now this. Everybody was right. I'd lost my dignity, my friends. I might lose my mother. All of that for Keith and he hadn't changed one bit.

"How could he do this to me?" I cried as I slumped to the floor.

I jumped when I felt a hand gently touch my shoulder. I looked up to see Angel kneeling in front of me. Alexis and Jasmine were right behind her. I looked at all three, waiting on somebody to light into me, begin telling me a bunch of "I told you so's."

"How much did you hear?" I whispered as I tried to wipe my eyes.

"Enough," Angel said with a sympathetic look on her face.

"He's with his baby's mama, ain't he?" Jasmine asked.

I slowly nodded. "He never broke up with her. He lied—again."

"It's going to be all right," Alexis said, taking my hand. "We're here for you and that's all that matters."

I looked at Jasmine.

Jasmine smiled. "Through thick and thin."

At that very moment I couldn't help but thank God for giving me such great friends. I laid my head on Alexis's shoulder and cried.

37

Angel

$\mathcal{C}$amille's mother had another surgery today and I really wanted to be there. But today was an important day. The day I would make the final arrangements to give up my child.

Rosario had dropped me off and taken the baby for a picture so that I would always have something to remember her by.

I tried my best to stay calm as I made my way inside my mother's house.

"Mami?" I called out.

"In the back," my mother responded.

I walked down the long hallway adorned with pictures from my childhood. My first birthday party. My *quinceañera*. Memories of happier times. Seeing all of these pictures used to make me smile. Not today, though.

I stepped into the kitchen. My mother was seated at the table with a stuffy-looking woman in a business suit.

The woman stood as I walked in.

"Angel, this is Miss Rogers, the lady I told you about," my mother said as I shook her hand.

"Nice to meet you, Angel. I've heard so much about you." The woman looked like the mean old foster care lady in that movie *Annie*. She wore her hair in a tight bun and her catwoman-looking glasses rested on the tip of her nose.

I forced a smile. What was I supposed to say to the woman who was about to take my baby away?

The woman looked around. "I thought you'd have the baby with you."

"She's with my sister," I replied.

The woman sat back down. "Mrs. Lopez, as I'm sure you are aware, the Adoption Angels program needs to be one hundred percent sure that the birth mother is okay with her decision to give up her child. Are you making this decision of your own free will?" She took out a notepad and started scribbling.

"I am," I said softly as I sat down across the table from the woman. I wondered if Miss Rogers could tell I was lying.

"See," my mother said. "We are sure."

"Well, as you know, the Hartfords have been screened and are anxiously awaiting the baby. And they would like to get their daughter as soon as possible. Preferably tomorrow," Miss Rogers said as she pushed her glasses up on her nose.

Their daughter? I fought back tears as I listened to the woman so easily give my baby to someone else.

"It's my understanding that the baby is going back to the hospital tomorrow for her three-week tests? How about we just have the Hartfords pick her up there?" Miss Rogers said.

"That's fine," my mother said, without giving me a chance to speak.

Miss Rogers stood. "We'll see you tomorrow, then. It's been a pleasure."

I stayed seated at the table as my mother walked Miss Rogers out. A few minutes later, my mother returned. I could feel her standing in the kitchen doorway staring at me, but I couldn't bring myself to look her in the eye.

"I know you're unsure of this decision, *mija*. But again, it's for the best. The child will be placed with someone who can love her."

"I love her."

My mother's expression softened. "Let me rephrase then. Someone who can provide for her. Can you do that?"

"Mami, we don't know anyone who has given their child up for adoption." I didn't know why I was pleading now. The decision had been made.

"I know, sweetheart. But we've talked about this. We are making this decision in the best interest of the baby and you. Just look at it this way. You can finish school, even go on to college."

"Okay, Mami. Whatever you say." I tried my best not to cry. It was the right decision. But that thought did nothing to ease the ache in my heart.

38

Angel

I read the name tag on the jolly-looking nurse. Nurse Louise. That sounded like somebody's grandmother. And that's just how the nurse was acting, especially the way she had been fussing over the baby since we'd arrived at the hospital.

Nurse Louise had taken the baby in for her tests and she was now back in the hospital conference room, trying to talk to me.

"I know I asked you this already," she said as she sat down next to me, "but I have to ask one more time. Are you sure you don't want to see her?"

I sat at the conference room table, a pink baby blanket clutched in my hand. When I'd handed Angelica to the nurse, I couldn't bear to let the blanket go. I needed to keep something to remind me of my baby.

"No, I . . . I'm sure. We just brought her in for her final checkup before we, you know, let her new family take her home." I had to force the words out. I had wanted to hand the baby over to the Hartfords myself, but Miss Rogers said it would make it too hard. So the couple was waiting in another conference room to pick up Angelica.

"Home should be with you," the nurse leaned in and whispered.

"I can't afford to keep her. And if I do keep her, I won't be able to give her the stuff she needs. She doesn't deserve that kind of life." I was surprised I wasn't crying again. Maybe it was because I was just all cried out.

"There's always a way, you remember that." The nurse gently touched my arm just as my mother walked back into the conference room from the restroom.

"Hello," my mother said. She looked happier than she had in days. I didn't understand how anyone could be thrilled about giving away their own flesh and blood.

The nurse squeezed my hand as she stood up. "Hello. I was just telling Angel here how beautiful her baby is."

My mother looked like she tensed up. "Have they finished testing?"

The nurse looked at my mother like she wanted to say something more. "They have. Let me go get the results to add to her paperwork. Then I guess we'll be all wrapped up and you can go on with your lives and your baby, I mean, the Hartfords' baby can go to her new home." Nurse Louise looked at me before stepping out of the room.

"Don't let her make you backtrack on this decision," my mother said when she caught me staring at the door. "We've already decided. There's no turning back. It's for the best."

I was sick of hearing that. I just wanted to get out of the hospital. I closed my eyes and leaned back. Why was my agony being prolonged? Why did I have to wait? Why couldn't I just leave? Why couldn't my mother disappear? Why couldn't everybody just leave me alone?

I was surprised when my mother stopped talking and sat in silence for a few minutes.

"You're doing the right thing. We're doing the right thing," she finally said. She looked sad herself. "You're just a baby yourself."

Nurse Louise walked back into the room. I quickly stood as my eyes made their way to the nurse's arms, where Angelica was wrapped in a thick baby blanket, fast asleep.

"What's going on?" my mother said as her eyes darted from the baby to the nurse. At that moment, the conference room door flew open and Miss Rogers came running into the room. "I am so sorry, we've never had anything like this happen," she said as she raced over to my mother.

"Anything like what? What's going on?" I asked, still trying to make sense of everything.

"The Hartfords have backed out. They've always wanted a baby boy, but were going to take Angelica because there were no boys available. They learned today that a boy is available for immediate adoption so they've changed their mind about Angelica," Miss Rogers said.

I was dazed. "What does that mean?"

"It means you can either take your darling baby girl home or she can go to a foster home," Nurse Louise said as she stepped forward with the baby.

I gasped. "A foster home?"

The nurse nodded.

I turned toward my mother, a look of desperation on my face. "Mami, I can't let her go to a foster home. You remember what happened to Ricardo?" A neighbor's son was sent to a foster home and he was abused so bad they arrested his foster parents.

Miss Rogers quickly stepped in. "Either situation would only be temporary, as our agency has plenty of willing families. We just have to locate one. And rest assured, they've been screened so you don't have to worry about your baby being harmed."

"Ricardo's foster family was screened," I pleaded to my mother, who was standing there with a stunned look on her face. She massaged her forehead.

"If—if she went to a home, how long would she be there?"

"Until we find her a permanent home," Miss Rogers replied. "Which I'm sure won't take long. There are so many people out there dying for a beautiful baby girl."

"How long?" my mother repeated.

"We can't make any promises," Miss Rogers softly replied.

"So you mean she may never be adopted?" I asked.

Miss Rogers looked apologetic. "Unfortunately, that's exactly what it means."

I stared at Miss Rogers. This wasn't part of the deal. The only reason I was giving my baby up for adoption was to give her a better life. A foster home was not a better life.

As if on cue, Angelica began cooing. I wanted to cry as I took my baby in my arms.

"Even if you take her home, it most likely will be just temporary," Miss Rogers continued. "I'm hopeful that we will be able to place her in an adoptive home pretty quickly."

My mother sank down in a chair. "What are we going to do?"

"Take your grandbaby home," Nurse Louise whispered.

I touched Angelica's face. It was so smooth. My baby girl stretched and yawned as she looked up at me. She was beautifully dressed in a white jumper with a matching hat trimmed in pink ribbon. It was an outfit from Camille, Alexis, and Jasmine. As I stared into her eyes, I knew there was no way I could give her up now.

"Mami, maybe this is a sign from God," I said as I caressed Angelica's face.

My mother sighed. "God does not approve of this. He does not condone teenagers having sex and making babies. But I guess we'll have to keep the baby for a while longer."

"Mrs. Lopez, I am so sorry," Miss Rogers said. "I assure you, if you take the baby home, it will only be for a short while. I have no doubt we'll find her a good home."

I wanted to turn a backflip. Now that Angelica was back in my arms, I knew this was exactly where my baby belonged. All I had to do was convince my mother of the same thing.

39

Angel

I watched as my mother fed Angelica and I couldn't help but smile at the way she stroked my daughter's hair. It had taken a week, but it was a sight I never thought I would see.

My mother had tried to be all hard the first few nights. She'd offered very little help. But then Angelica had smiled at her. My mother had tried to play it off, saying it was gas, but I could tell it had gotten to her.

Things were so much better since we were at my mother's house, in a nice, cozy bed. I found myself saying nightly prayers that my mother would come around completely and want my baby to stay.

My mother caught me staring at her. "Angel, come, come," she said, motioning for me to take a seat.

I slowly walked into the room. I hated that I had disturbed the rare moment of tenderness between my mother and baby.

"She is beautiful, isn't she?" I asked.

My mother had tears in her eyes as she continued staring at Angelica. "She looks just like the baby pictures of my sister."

I knew I was taking a chance, but I had to at least give it

a try. "Mami, what do we do if Miss Rogers can't find a family for her?"

My mother hesitated. "They will." For once, though, she didn't sound so sure.

As if on cue, Angelica smiled again and my mother's eyes lit up. But just as suddenly, her expression darkened. She stood up and pushed the baby toward me. "Here, take her."

I stood and took my daughter into my arms. Angelica continued making gurgling baby sounds. "She does look like Auntie Rosie, doesn't she," I said as my mother busied herself cleaning up the house. "I'm sure going to miss her."

My mother grabbed a dust rag and began wiping down the coffee table.

"You think the family that gets her will be good to her?" I knew I was messing with my mother, but I could tell I was getting to her.

"Better than you can," my mother said without looking up.

I ignored her comment. "What do you think she'll be when she grows up, Mami? You think she'll be a doctor, or maybe the first woman president of the United States?"

My mother pounded the table. "Stop it, *mija*! I know what you are doing." She stood up. "You think just because this baby is here, I will change my mind about her?" My mother walked over to the window and stared out.

With the baby still cuddled in my arms, I slowly walked toward her. "Mami, do you really want to give her away?"

My mother turned around and faced me. "Of course I don't want to give her away! I just put it out there as an option for us to consider. And the more I thought about it, the more I convinced myself it was the answer. Then when God sent the Hartfords, I took that as a sign." My mother paused and took a deep breath. "This is hard for me, too. I was trying to do what was best for everyone, but I don't know what I'm doing either, *mija*. And maybe"—she paused and looked at Angelica—"just maybe she is meant to be with us. This was not the life I had planned for you, but it is the one God has chosen for you. For us." She exhaled again and looked at me. "If you are going to raise this child, I don't want to hear any complaints. There is no going out with your friends, no parties, no hanging out, no sitting up on the phone. Just school, work, and taking care of this child. And you will follow my rule of no boys. You have made one mistake, you will not make another. If you cannot abide by my rules, you will have to go. Do you understand me?"

It took a minute for everything my mother was saying to register. I stared at her in disbelief. "What are you saying, Mami?" I repeated.

My mother went back to dusting, this time wiping down the piano that sat in the corner of our living room. "I'm not saying anything. I'm just telling you, don't think you're going to give me the baby and just go running the streets. Angelica will be *your* responsibility."

"Does this mean we don't have to go through with the adoption?" I was on pins and needles, but I still had to be sure. "And me and the baby can stay?"

My mother wiped harder and faster. "You will get a job immediately. And you will pay for your own daycare, and your own food, and your own everything. You want to be grown and have a child, you will be grown and take care of it." She stopped wiping and stood up. When she turned to face me again, tears had returned to her eyes. "But, yes, you and Angelica can stay. She's family. I can't turn my back on family." My mother shook her finger. "This does not change my disappointment in you."

I had to fight back tears myself. "I know, Mami. I am so sorry. But I will make it up to you. I will make you proud of me. I will make you and my baby proud. Thank you."

My mother glared at me like she wanted to say something more. Finally, she did something I never thought she'd do. She opened her arms and pulled me and her granddaughter into a big hug.

40

Camille

I smiled as Angelica tried desperately to put her tiny fingers in her mouth.

"She is so cute," I said.

"Yeah, but we'd better get going before she wakes up your mother," Angel responded.

I looked toward my mother's bedroom. She had been home three days and was now recovering in her own bed. She had pulled through surgery and, to everyone's surprise, was doing remarkably well considering all that she'd been through. She wasn't completely out of the woods yet, but she was well enough to come home.

"How are you managing taking care of her?" Jasmine asked as she propped her legs up on the coffee table in our living room. All four of us were gathered at my house to celebrate Angel's news that her mother was allowing her to keep her baby.

"The hospital is giving her an around-the-clock nurse. So we'll manage. Besides, my mother has been taking care of me for so long, I don't think a few weeks of me doing the same will kill me," I said.

All three of the girls stared at me before Alexis turned to

Jasmine. "Did she just say something nice about her mother?"

"I wouldn't have believed it if I didn't hear it with my own ears," Jasmine said.

"Ha, ha, ha. Very funny," I laughed.

"Naw, I'm just surprised, that's all," Jasmine said. "You know you ain't never showed your mother no love."

The smile left my face. "You're right. If anything, all I ever did was stress her out. That's probably why she ended up in the hospital in the first place."

"Come on," Angel said. "You know this wasn't your fault."

"Why not? The doctor said not only was she already sick, but stress made her sicker. And Lord knows I did nothing but stress her out," I responded.

"Well, now that that idiot boyfriend of yours is gone, we don't have to worry about that anymore," Jasmine said.

Everyone turned toward Jasmine.

"Do you have no class?" Alexis snapped.

"Yeah, Jasmine, why'd you have to go there?" Angel said.

Jasmine shrugged. "Y'all know I tell it like it is."

"Well, you don't—"

"Stop it." I cut off Alexis before she could get Jasmine riled up and the two of them spent the next thirty minutes arguing. "Jasmine is right. My relationship with Keith nearly killed my mother. And he wasn't even worth it."

Jasmine shot Alexis an "I told you so" look.

Angel reached down and pulled her baby out of the infant car seat. "Speaking of Keith, have you even heard from him?" She laid the baby across her lap and began patting her back.

"He's been calling me nonstop, but truthfully, I'm just

trying to focus on my mother. I'm not trying to hear any of his lies."

"Good. That's where your attention needs to be focused anyway," Jasmine said as she walked over to check out some pictures on the fireplace mantel.

The doorbell rang before I could respond.

"You want me to get it?" Jasmine asked since she was right next to the door.

"Yeah. It's probably just my mother's nurse."

Jasmine looked out the peephole and sucked her teeth.

"What? Who is it?" Alexis asked.

"He must've known we were talking about him," Jasmine groaned.

"It's Keith?" Alexis asked.

I didn't know what to say. How could he even have the audacity to show his face?

"Camille, open the door. I know you're in there. I hear voices," Keith yelled through the door.

Jasmine jerked the door open. "Do you see dead people, too?"

Keith looked at her, and snarled, "Where's Camille?"

"Busy." Jasmine moved to slam the door, but Keith stuck his foot in the door.

"Can you tell her I'm here to see her?"

Jasmine opened the door and placed her hands on her hips. "Let's see, when she didn't return any of your four hundred calls, did you not get the message?"

Keith rolled his eyes at Jasmine. "Look, you big—"

Alexis stepped in the doorway before he could finish his sentence. "If I were you, I wouldn't say that. My girl here doesn't play and she will definitely make you regret that."

Keith turned his lip up. "I ain't scared of your girl. Or

you. Or anyone else for that matter. Now where's *my* girl?"

"Your girl is probably at home with your son. Why don't you go join them?" Alexis said.

"Why don't all of you mind your own business?" Keith muttered. "Camille!" he yelled over Jasmine's shoulder.

"Stop hollering, you stupid idiot," Angel said, joining them in the doorway. "Her mother is sick and she doesn't need you out here causing problems."

"Just go get Camille."

"Just go home," Jasmine replied.

"No, Jasmine, let him in." I stood in the middle of the living room with my arms crossed over my chest.

Jasmine turned and looked at me in amazement. "You've got to be kidding me? I know you're not going to fall for this bs again?"

"Just let him in."

Jasmine rolled her eyes as she stepped out of the way.

Keith smirked as he strutted past Jasmine and into the foyer. I was trying extremely hard not to go off.

"Hey, boo," Keith said as he reached out and tried to pull me into his arms. "How's your mom?"

I broke free from his grasp. "Oh, so *now* you wanna know?"

"Don't be like that, Camille." Keith put on his best puppy dog look.

Jasmine slammed the door. "Where's your baby mama?"

Keith ignored her, keeping his attention focused on me. "Baby, I can explain everything. If you'll just get rid of these lonely, can't-get-their-own-man-so-they-wanna-mess-with-yours girls, we can work this all out."

"I know you didn't," Jasmine said as she stepped toward him, ready to fight.

Angel grabbed her arm, stopping her. "Jasmine, chill."

"Yeah, Jasmine, chill," I said without taking my eyes off Keith. "Keith here knows that I'm so madly in love with him that he can just show up here after a week and everything is straight."

"Naw, baby, it ain't even like that. I wanted to give you time to calm down so I could explain to you what really happened," Keith said, trying to sound sincere.

I kept my arms folded as I nodded my head. "Explain? Oh, okay. I knew you had a good excuse for lying to me again."

"I do, baby," Keith pleaded. "Just gimme a chance to explain."

Jasmine cocked her head. "Are you falling for this again? I don't believe this."

Keith smirked again. "Believe it, tramp."

Jasmine looked like she was about to lose it. Angel grabbed her arm just as she took a step toward Keith. "Oh, it's about to be on for real," Jasmine said, snatching her arm from Angel's grip.

"Jasmine, I will ask you one more time, chill," I calmly said. "I want to hear him out."

Keith put his arm around my neck as Jasmine huffed and stomped off. "Bet. See, what y'all don't understand," he said, looking at Alexis, Jasmine, and Angel, "is that what me and my girl have is bond. You can't break it. Nobody can."

Keith leaned in and tried to kiss me on the cheek. I pulled away. "Bond? That is so funny," I laughed. "Bond? I guess *bond* is what sent you to LaShay's house and kept you there when I needed you most."

"It's not even like that, baby."

I held my hands up to stop him as he stepped closer to me. "You know what, Keith? My mama is always telling me she didn't raise no fool. And she's right. I was a fool behind you long enough, but not anymore."

"Camille, you letting your girls fill your head with all this drama—"

I cut him off. "No, I let you fill my head." I poked him in the chest. "I kicked my girls to the curb for you and you know what, they were still there when I needed them. That, baby, is bond."

Alexis, Jasmine, and Angel stepped up next to me. Alexis draped her arm through mine and stared at Keith.

"Oh, so it's like that?" Keith asked.

"And then some," I responded coldly.

Jasmine stepped toward Keith, towering over him. "Now, as you would say, beat it."

Keith looked like he was contemplating what to do. He finally shrugged and said, "It ain't nothing but a thang. I was trying to do you a favor," he told me. "You'll be back."

"I wouldn't hold my breath," I responded.

We all laughed as Keith walked out the door. And I knew I finally had him out of my system.

41

Angel

The sounds of "Joy to the World" filled the small meeting room at Zion Hill Missionary Baptist Church. Although it was unusually warm for December—74 degrees—there was still a festive atmosphere throughout the room.

We had spent the past hour hanging Christmas decorations, moving furniture, and setting up the food for the Good Girlz Christmas reception scheduled to get under way in less than ten minutes.

I was standing at the top of the ladder, trying my best not to fall. I held out my hands to steady myself. "Whoa . . ."

"Would you chill? I got you," Jasmine said.

I looked down at Jasmine, who had both hands gripped firmly around the ladder. I saw Jasmine's reassuring look and my worries went out the window. It was funny how in just six months I had come to trust Jasmine and the others like I had known them my whole life.

"Just put the angel up there already," Jasmine snapped playfully. Jasmine could try and act mean all she wanted, but I knew now it was just that, an act.

I leaned in and placed the delicate ceramic angel on top of the tree. "There. I'm coming down."

Jasmine held the ladder steady while I grabbed hold of the sides and eased my way down.

"Isn't she beautiful?" I said as we looked up at the angel.

"You know, she kinda reminds me of you," Alexis said as she walked up. She looked too cute in a red satin wrap dress and black snakeskin boots. Her hair, as usual, was bouncing and behaving.

"Oh, God, y'all are so corny," Jasmine moaned.

"No, she does. For real," Alexis said. "Look at the eyes." Everybody stared up at the angel. Her eyes were almond shaped and a deep brown, just like mine.

"Nope, just don't see it," Jasmine said, shaking her head.

"She's just mad because she wants you to say how beautiful she is, too," Camille joked as she walked back in the room with a box she had gone to retrieve from the kitchen.

"Hey, I told y'all, no dress jokes," Jasmine threatened.

All three of us laughed. Jasmine had shocked everyone when she walked in with a tight, burgundy, knee-length, long-sleeved dress. It showed off curves no one even knew she had. She even had on earrings and a small silver necklace. Her long hair was back in its signature ponytail, but at least this time it was wrapped in a nice bun.

"Jasmine, you know you look gorgeous, darling," Alexis laughed.

"Shut up," Jasmine replied as she pulled at her panty hose.

"See, that's why you can't give some people compliments," Alexis joked.

"What made you wear a dress?" Camille asked. "I mean, it looks good. I'm just shocked, that's all."

"More like who. My granny is bringing all my relatives

and she made me wear this stupid thing. I don't know what the big deal is. It's just a reception. It's not like we're graduating from high school or something." Jasmine wiggled like the dress was making her uncomfortable.

"Girl, you know since Miss Rachel has us all making a speech about how God has blessed our lives, my mama is acting like this is more important than graduation," Camille said.

"I still don't understand why we gotta get up in front of everybody and talk, especially to give some stupid speech about how blessed we are," Jasmine whined.

"Because you are blessed and we want everyone to know it," Rachel said as she entered the room. A big smile crossed her face. "You all have made tremendous strides in not only your relationships with each other, but also your relationships with God—and that's reason to celebrate."

Rachel playfully pinched Jasmine's cheek. "You know I am so proud of you girls." She looked around the room. "And you all have done such a wonderful job decorating this room."

"Yeah, we wanted the reception to be really nice," Alexis said as she hung another string of garland across the window. Besides the seven-foot tree and garlands across all the windows, there were angels of all races and other multicultural ornaments positioned all around the room. The front podium had beautiful red ribbons hanging from it.

"I love Christmastime," Rachel said. "When I was growing up, my mom used to go crazy at Christmas. She would buy us so much stuff and my daddy would always fuss, but he never made her take any of the stuff back."

"I wish I could've met your mother," I said as I sat down to massage my feet, which were killing me from the high heels I now regretted wearing. "She seemed like she was really nice."

"She was. I just didn't appreciate her until she was gone."

"How did your mom die?" Camille asked.

Rachel's eyes got watery. "She had a heart attack when I was nineteen. I always wonder if me and my brothers hadn't made her life so hard, would her heart have given in. It's like the stress of dealing with our problems made her heart weak." Rachel gazed out the window as the room grew silent.

I stared at Camille, who had started getting glossy-eyed herself. I wondered if Camille was thinking the same thing I was. We'd both come a long way with our relationships with our mothers. And while I hadn't come close to physically losing my mother like Camille had, I'd almost lost her out of my life.

Rachel seemed to snap out of the daze she was in. "Look at me. This is not a sad occasion. Today is a good day. This is a celebration of how far we've come. Your families are coming and we are here to celebrate the progress you've made! My niece Tameka will even be here. I wanted her to come to see what she missed out on. Hopefully, she'll join us next year. Because I know each of you will be back, right?"

"Of course," Camille said.

"You know I'm in," Alexis added.

"You're all like my family, so I'm not going anywhere," I said with a big grin.

"Do I have any choice?" Jasmine groaned, before cracking a smile.

"I hate to interrupt this tender moment here." Everyone turned toward Rachel's husband, Rev. Adams, who had just walked into the room. "But I wanted to see if you guys were ready."

"Hi, honey. We're good to go," Rachel replied. She started waving when she saw Tameka walk in. Tameka waved back before taking a seat in the back of the room. I wondered if we should go over and speak, but judging from the look on Tameka's face, she seemed like she really didn't want to be bothered. I waved anyway. Tameka barely waved back.

I turned my attention back to Rev. Adams, who was looking around the room. "Wow, you all have done a good job," he said.

"Thank you," Alexis responded.

"And we're ready just in time, because Angel, here comes your mother and sister," Rachel said.

I turned toward the door where my mother slowly walked in pushing a baby stroller, Angelica sleeping soundly inside. Rosario and her daughters were behind them.

"Angel, this is so nice," Rosario said as she scanned the room.

"Thank you. I'm glad you all came." I hugged my sister and toussled my nieces' hair before turning to my mother. "I'm especially glad you're here, Mami."

"I'm glad I'm here, too, *mija*," my mother responded with a smile.

I leaned down and kissed my daughter before leading my family to their seats at the front. The room was starting to fill up with some other people I didn't know, probably other people from Zion Hill.

I watched as a tall woman who looked like she was a man in another life wheeled in Camille's mother. Even though Mrs. Harris was confined to a wheelchair, she looked healthy and in good spirits.

Camille walked over to greet her mother, who wore a proud look.

"I can't wait to hear your speech," her mother said as she squeezed her daughter's hand. "I'm just so happy my prayers have been answered. Just the fact that this group has you talking about blessings is a blessing in itself."

"Oh, Mama," Camille groaned, but this time at least she had a smile across her face.

A few minutes later, a large group of people walked into the room. There had to be at least twenty of them. "Oh, Lord, look at my baby. Ain't she just beautiful?"

I wouldn't have known who the woman was if I hadn't heard Jasmine groan and roll her eyes. The way the elderly woman was fussing over her, that had to be Jasmine's grandmother.

The woman walked over and pulled Jasmine into a bear hug. "My baby is growing up," she cried. "Ooooh, she's just so beautiful."

"Granny, please," Jasmine said.

"I can't help it. I'm just so happy." Jasmine's grandmother turned toward the group and motioned to several of the kids in the front. "Y'all come look at your sister. Don't she look cute?"

"Ewww, I ain't never seen you in no dress," one of the little boys said.

Me and Camille laughed. Jasmine pushed the little boy's shoulder. "Shut up, boy," Jasmine said.

"He's right, though," Camille whispered to me as we both tried not to laugh.

"Where's Mama?" Jasmine asked.

"Parking the car. She'll be right in," her grandmother said as she looked at the table covered with food. "I hope y'all got more than these little finger sandwiches. These kids is hungry."

No sooner had she said that than two little boys made their way to the table and began grabbing the little sand- wiches and stuffing them into their mouths. Another teenaged boy was next to them grabbing a handful of potatos chips.

"Jaquan, Jalen, and Jaheim, get your tails over here right now!" Jasmine's grandmother walked over and snatched the two boys by the arm. "Acting like you ain't got no home training."

"They don't," a tall, slender girl with long braids said.

"Don't start with me today, Nikki," Jasmine's grand- mother snapped.

"Dang!" Jasmine said. "Can y'all please not start this?"

I watched as another woman, who had to be Jasmine's mother, made her way into the room. The woman looked just like Jasmine.

"Now I see where Jasmine gets her height," Camille whispered to me. The woman had to be at least six-two.

"Hey, Mama," Jasmine said.

"Hey. Is this little shindig 'bout to get started? I got to get to work. I thought this thing was supposed to start at two. See, even the church is on CP time." Her mother had a look like she'd been forced to come as well. Jasmine took a deep breath.

"We'll get started in just a minute, Mama. Can you please have a seat?" Jasmine said through clenched teeth.

Jasmine's mother motioned for her family to take their seats in the second row.

"Can't we eat first?" Jalen whined.

"Boy, shut up and wait," his mother said.

Jasmine eased back over to us. "Now you see why I don't ever want to go home. I gotta deal with that every day." Her chipper mood had turned sour.

I wanted to offer some comforting words but I didn't know what to say. Alexis was the positive one in the group. Maybe she could get Jasmine's spirits back up.

"Where's Alexis?" I whispered to Camille.

"I don't know," Camille responded. We looked around the room and spotted Alexis gazing out the window.

We walked over to her. "Hey, are you looking for your parents?" Camille asked.

Alexis nodded. "My mom, anyway. My dad can't make it because he had a meeting. He always has a meeting." Alexis seemed to be talking to herself. "And, of course, my mother is late."

"Do you want me to get Miss Rachel to stall to give her time to get here?" Camille asked.

"Naw. I know my mom, there's no telling what time she'll get here. If she gets here at all. But I'm used to it." Alexis tried to act like it was no big deal as she put a smile on her face. "It's fifteen minutes after two anyway. Let's go ahead and get started."

We made our way to our seats as Rev. Adams walked up to the podium. After a short prayer, Rachel came up and gave a brief background on the program and how well each of us had done. Then one by one we took the podium and gave our speeches. My mother was beaming with pride as I talked about the day I stumbled onto the church grounds, looking for an answer to my problem.

". . . I never expected God to lead me where I am today, but He did. And that's how I know for a fact that I'm truly blessed," I said as I finished up my speech.

After I went, Camille, Alexis, and Jasmine all gave equally great five-minute speeches. Camille's mother had tears in her eyes as Camille finished and Jasmine's grandmother wouldn't stop bawling, talking about, "That's my baby!"

After they wrapped up, Rachel returned to the podium. She also had tears in her eyes as she gave each of us a certificate of appreciation and a five-hundred-dollar savings bond, compliments of the church.

"Thank you all for coming," Rachel said as we returned to our seats. "Please, enjoy refreshments and know that your daughters are making you proud. Please join me in giving them a round of applause."

All of us stood and turned around as the audience clapped. We were all beaming.

After mingling with the crowd and watching Jasmine's siblings devour the food, I was ready to get going. I headed over to Camille.

"You want to leave?" Camille whispered.

"Yeah, we can go ahead and go to the hotel," I said. Rachel had gotten us a hotel suite for the night to have a celebratory slumber party.

"And you know I'm ready to go get out of this dang dress anyway," Jasmine said.

Alexis laughed.

"Let me just tell my family," Jasmine added.

"Me, too," Camille and I said in unison.

Camille turned to Alexis. "You want to go on to your car?" she asked. "I'll grab your stuff and we'll be out in a minute."

Alexis nodded and eased out the side door. We all walked over to the table where our mothers were standing, said our good-byes, and headed out for our own celebration.

42

Camille

It had taken hours' worth of begging, but Jasmine had finally given in. I couldn't believe she'd finally agreed to let us make her over.

We were in a suite at the Hilton Americas Hotel. Rachel was in the room next door, getting some "much needed rest and relaxation," as she put it. Alexis had spent the first hour or so down in the dumps because her mom was a no-show. But when Angel popped out her sister's copy of *The Best of American Idol,* Alexis started acting like her old self. We watched the worst singers part twice before kicking back and pigging out on pizza. After we each had more than our share, Alexis had suggested we give Jasmine a makeover.

Of course, Jasmine had been totally against the idea, but had finally given in when it was evident that Alexis wasn't giving up.

"This is so stupid," Jasmine said as Alexis pushed her down in a chair.

"Would you just be quiet and let us work our magic," I said as I plugged my curling iron into the outlet, then draped a towel around Jasmine's neck.

"I just don't understand what the big deal is," Jasmine said. "Why do you guys want me in all that makeup? Plus, it's not like we're about to go out anywhere. We're just going to bed."

"It's not a bunch of makeup," Alexis said as she began laying out all of her MAC makeup on the dresser. "It's just enough to enhance your natural beauty. And we don't have to be going anywhere. We're just having fun."

"There's nothing fun about this." Jasmine frowned. She scowled even more when I lifted her ponytail. "What are we going to do about this?" I asked.

"I say chop it off," Angel joked.

Jasmine quickly jumped up. "I don't think so."

Alexis gently pushed her back down in the seat. "Chill out. She was just kidding."

"Yeah, ain't nobody fixin' to cut your hair," I said. I reached to pull the rubber band off. Jasmine moved her head out of my reach.

"Would you be still?" I said.

Jasmine looked at me skeptically. "You don't need to touch my hair. I happen to like my ponytail."

"We know," I laughed. "You wear it every single day. I don't think we've ever seen you with it down."

"And it's so pretty and thick," Angel said as I eased the rubber band off Jasmine's ponytail.

"Trust us, Jazzy. You'll love the new you," Alexis said.

Jasmine rolled her eyes. "Jazzy? My name is Jasmine."

"Whatever," Alexis said.

"Look, I'm letting y'all change my look. You're not about to change my name, too," Jasmine snapped.

"Fine, Jasmine," I said. "Just sit back, relax, and let us do our thang."

Jasmine groaned as she leaned back in the chair. Alexis went to work on her makeup, while I started combing and curling her hair. Angel went through Alexis's makeup case and pulled out some pink nail polish. She reached for Jasmine's hands.

"Where do you think you're going with that?" Jasmine said.

Angel grabbed her hand. "You said you would let us do this."

"No pink," Jasmine firmly said.

"Good grief," Angel said as she started digging in the makeup case again. "How's this beige then?" she said as she held up a small bottle of nail polish.

"That's fine," Jasmine replied.

We went to work on Jasmine.

"Jasmine, you know you never did tell us your story," I said as I put the finishing touches on her hair. "We've been here all this time and no one really knows a whole lot about you."

"And no one needs to know," Jasmine said.

"That's not fair," Alexis said. "Do your lips like this," she told Jasmine as she rubbed her lips together.

Jasmine repeated the action. "Life isn't fair. Besides, nobody wants to hear my boring story."

"Yes, we do," Angel said, blowing on Jasmine's nails.

"And with your family, it seems like things are anything but boring," I said.

Jasmine finally laughed. "You got that right. Maybe one day I'll tell y'all all about them, about all the crazy stuff I've been through with them. But for now," she said as she stood up, "I need to see what type of monster y'all have turned me into." Jasmine tried to turn toward the mirror. I caught her.

"Wait." I grabbed her shoulders to keep her from turning around. "Everybody ready?"

Angel and Alexis nodded.

"Okay. Presenting, the new, improved, and absolutely stunning Jasmine Jones." I slowly turned Jasmine around to face the mirror.

We stood in silence as Jasmine looked at her reflection. I expected her to start going off at any moment. Jasmine's eyes got wide. "Wow." She fluffed her hair, then leaned in closer to see her face.

"So, you like?" Alexis asked proudly.

Jasmine slowly straighened. "It's a'ight." She smiled.

"A'ight?" I said. "Girl, you are all that and a bag of chips."

"Yeah," Angel added. "You look like . . . like a girl."

We all broke out in laughter.

Jasmine turned up her lips before breaking out in a big smile. "Okay, I am fly, ain't I?"

All three of us squealed in delight as we leaned in and hugged Jasmine. Jasmine turned back toward the mirror. "I look kinda cute, man."

"I told you," I said. "Now stop saying 'man.' You sound like a dude."

Jasmine turned to face us. Her expression turned serious. "You know y'all my girls, right? I mean, I haven't had anyone I would consider a real friend in a long time. And I'm . . . well, I'm just glad y'all are my friends." Jasmine sounded like she was choking up. She looked away quickly.

"Oh, my God. You gon' make me cry," Alexis said.

I stared at Jasmine. Never in a million years did I think those words would come out of her mouth. "You know when I started in this group, I didn't want to be here," I said.

"Shoot, you?" Jasmine said, turning back to face us. "Angel was the only one who wanted to be here."

"Because I knew it was a good thing," Angel said with a big smile.

"Yeah, everything happens for a reason," I responded. "And whatever brought us together, let's promise to stay friends forever." I reached out and took Angel's hands.

"Friends."

"To the end," Angel responded as she took Alexis's hand.

"Forever," Alexis said. She took Jasmine's hand. Everyone looked at Jasmine.

"What?" she replied.

"You're supposed to say something sweet," Alexis said.

"Gimme a break. Enough with the mushy stuff," Jasmine said.

"You started it," I replied. "And we're not finishing until you complete the friendship pact. Again, girls. Friends."

"To the end," Angel added.

"Forever." Alexis smiled and turned to Jasmine.

"Y'all are the corniest people I have ever seen in my life," Jasmine said.

"Jasmine!" all three of us yelled.

"Okay, okay." Jasmine smiled. "And ever."

"Did that kill you?" I asked.

"Almost," Jasmine replied.

I smiled as I reached out and hugged my friends. I'd come a long way with the Good Girlz, and while it seemed like my life had been nothing but drama, I knew the one thing I could always count on was my girls to help me work it out.

Reading Group Guide for
Nothing But Drama

A Conversation with ReShonda Tate Billingsley

Q: *Nothing But Drama* is the first in a series of Christian teen novels, each having one of the Ten Commandments as its theme. Why did you choose to begin with "honor thy mother and father"? Also, why do you think spirituality is so important for today's youth?

A: Believe it or not, honoring one's parents is probably the simplest of the commandments, yet for teens it can be the hardest. Teens are just starting to figure out who they are (or at least who they think they are) and parents represent the notion that they are still children. While writing, I thought back to my own challenges with my mother. Back then, there was no way I would have ever thought I'd someday thank her for the things she did to and for me.

Spirituality is important because it sets the foundation for life and the decisions we make as adults. There is an old adage that goes, "Train up a child in the way they should go, and he will rarely depart from it." When young people have a strong foundation, as they become adults, they generally don't stray from it.

Q: How do you teach the same values you write about in your books to your own daughters?

A: First and foremost, I try to live by example. It amazes me how many of my ways and mannerisms my daughters pick up from me. I teach my daughters by talking to them—a lot.

I want them to always feel safe to come and discuss any issue with me. I sit with them and discuss right from wrong so they have a firm understanding of what is acceptable and what is not. When all is said and done, I leave them with a clear message: I ain't your friend. I'm your mama.

Q: All of your novels have been book club selections, and you have often been invited to attend book club meetings across the country. What aspects of your books do you think make them the perfect book club read?

A: I may be a writer, but I'm also a reader. And I know what I like in a book—a story that keeps me turning the pages, characters I care about, and topics that spark discussion. So basically, that's what I put in my own writing. My goal is to create realistic characters who are experiencing the same things readers deal with in their own lives. That way, whenever a group of people get together to discuss my books, the conversation can include what is going on in their own lives.

Q: Why did you decide to self-publish your debut novel, *My Brother's Keeper*? What did this experience teach you and what advice do you have for aspiring writers?

A: I knew that I had a good story to tell. I was just having a hard time convincing agents and publishers of that. After learning that an agent I had submitted my manuscript to rejected it without ever looking at it, I decided to not let anyone but me and my God determine my destiny. I didn't want to sit around and wait on someone to validate my talents. I researched and learned how to publish my book myself. The experience confirmed what I already knew—I could do anything I set my mind to. My advice to other writers is to always determine your own destiny, keep writing, and don't take "no" for an answer.

Q: Why did you bring back Rachel Jackson, first introduced in *Let the Church Say Amen,* in your new teen series? What is it about Rachel that makes her an ideal leader of the Good Girlz? Is she based on anyone you know?

A: I had so much fun with Rachel. She got to do the outrageous things I was never brave enough to do (or will ever admit to doing). She was not based on one person, but on a lot of different people rolled into one. I chose her because no one would believe she was capable of leading a group of teenage girls (at least without a bunch of drama). But at the same time, I felt she would be more empathetic toward the girls, having been a wild teen herself. And who better to tell you what path *not* to take than someone who has traveled down that road herself. Leading the Good Girlz provides a good opportunity for her to show her growth as a woman.

Q: You write about real-world teen issues, from friendships to boyfriend trouble to problems at home. Do you write from personal experiences? How did you prepare to write a novel for teens that truly hits home?

A: While I won't admit to any of the Good Girlz drama mirroring my own, I do write from personal experiences—a bit of my own, a bit of my friends and family, and a bit of people I encounter on a day-to-day basis. I throw all that together with an active imagination, and I come up with stories. Even though this is fiction, I firmly believe in making my characters true to life—this is crucial in crafting a novel that truly hits home. And the best way to do that is to recall my experiences as a teen, talk to other teens, and try to stay in touch with young people.

Q: What is one of the most memorable things a fan has said to you?

A: When someone tells me my books touched or changed their life, or caused them to look at things differently, it makes everything I do worthwhile. At an event where I was a guest speaker, I met a young lady who said she hated reading—until she read my book. Now she not only reads my novels, but she reads any book she can get her hands on. It doesn't get any better than that.

Questions for Discussions

1. One of the major themes in *Nothing But Drama* is the clash between individuality and respect for a parent's wishes. When Camille is arrested for harboring her fugitive boyfriend in her grandmother's house, she says, "My mother was going to kill me for sure." Despite her fear of punishment, why does Camille continue to defy her mother and see Keith? How do you think Camille's mother could communicate more effectively with her?

2. Camille's mother shows her a newspaper article about Keith being found at the home of his girlfriend . . . who is also the mother of his child. Why is Camille resentful of her mother showing her the article? Cite instances where the generation gap between Camille and her mother is apparent.

3. After Camille's mother reads her journal and learns that she's still seeing Keith, she states, "When you start paying bills around here, then you can have some privacy." Do you agree with this? What does Camille learn after her mother suffers a heart attack? How does this put everything into perspective?

4. Angel is initially interested in Good Girlz because of the $25 raffle. Camille tells her, "This is my first time here. I'm just coming because I didn't have a choice." When all the girls agree to give Angel the money instead of participating in the drawing, it shows that not everything in their lives is out of their control. In what other instances throughout the novel do they exhibit the power of choice?

5. Rachel Adams, the First Lady of Zion Hill and the founder of the Good Girlz, admits, "It takes a lot of effort for me to walk the straight and narrow." Why do you think she shares her personal story and invites the girls to her happy home? What is she trying to show them?

6. Alexis comes from a wealthy family and appears to have the perfect life, but she has a mentally challenged sister whom her mother tries to hide. Rachel says, "We may not always understand our parents' motives, but it's important to respect their places in our lives." At what point in the story do the girls see for themselves how dysfunctional Alexis's family is? What do they learn about their own families?

7. Angel's mother convinces her to give her baby daughter up for adoption, but the adoption couple decides they want a baby boy instead. If fate hadn't intervened, would Angel have been true to herself and stood up to her mom? How will raising her own baby redefine Angel's relationship with her own mother? What do you think she will learn?

8. When you first meet Jasmine, she's the bulldog of the group, always picking a fight and intimidating the others. How does Jasmine change as the story progresses? Why do you think she's afraid to show her inner femininity and vulnerability in the beginning? How does she feel about boys? Discuss her relationship with her grandmother and how it helps define her.

9. When the girls find out that Angel is running away to Mexico, they follow her to bring her home. What does this say about their shift in priorities? At this point in the story, how has each girl changed for the better since she first joined Good Girlz?

10. Camille often asks that God not judge her and asks for His forgiveness. "I hoped God was as forgiving as Miss Rachel always claimed He was because I needed Him now more than ever." How does Camille's growing bond with God affect other relationships in her life? Do you think the girls changed for God . . . themselves . . . or someone else in their lives?

Activities to Enhance Your Book Club

Follow in the Good Girlz's footsteps and give back to your community. Check out Youth Service America at www.ysa.org where you can get involved in volunteer opportunities like fighting childhood hunger.

How well do you and your fellow book club members know each other? Write a multiple choice quiz about your favorite things—like food, movies, singers—then team up and see how many questions your fellow reader can get right.

Interview a parent, grandparent, aunt or uncle about what he/she was like as a teenager, and then share the results at your next meeting. Some of the stories might surprise you!

If you enjoyed *Nothing But Drama*, don't miss

Blessings
in
Disguise

Coming soon from POCKET BOOKS

Turn the page for a sneak preview . . .

$\mathcal{I}$ was the first to arrive to tonight's Good Girlz meeting. I couldn't wait for Angel and Camille to get here so I could tell them about Alexis and Trina.

I had wanted to call them over the weekend, but since our phone was cut off until the fifteenth, that wasn't possible. Just another reason why I wished I had a cell phone. It seemed like our phone got cut off every other month. And when it was working, my oldest sister Nikki was always on it. So I'd asked for a cell phone for my birthday. My grandmother had almost choked from laughter.

I paced back and forth across the meeting room, wishing they'd hurry up. Angel and Camille usually came to the meetings together. I was just about to go wait in the parking lot when both of them came bouncing into the room.

"What took y'all so long?" I asked.

"Huh?" Angel said. "What time is it?"

Camille looked at her watch. "It's only 6:30. We're not late. What are you talking about?"

I blew out a frustrated breath, peeked down the hall, then shut the door.

"What is wrong with you?" Camille asked.

"Yeah, and why are you here so early? You're always the last to arrive," Angel added.

"You two are not going to believe this," I said.

"What?" both of them said at the same time.

"I went to the mall with Alexis and Trina this weekend," I began.

"You're right," Camille interrupted. "I don't believe you, of all people, were hanging with Alexis and Trina. And at the mall nonetheless." Both she and Angel started laughing.

"Would you two stop cracking jokes? This is serious," I chastised.

They could both see I wasn't kidding because the smiles left their faces. Since I had their undivided attention, I continued. "When we left the mall and got back to the car, Trina pulled clothes out of her shirt, clothes she had stolen from the mall."

"You are lying," Camille said, her eyes wide.

"If I'm lying, I'm flying," I responded.

"Alexis doesn't steal. She doesn't need to," Angel said, as if the idea itself was absurd.

"That's the same thing I said. She didn't actually take anything but she knew what Trina was doing." I leaned in and lowered my voice. "I think they've been doing it a while. And get this—I think they may be getting ready to sell the stuff."

"Jasmine, you must've misunderstood—" Camille stopped mid-sentence and all of us turned toward the door as it slowly opened.

"Hey, everybody. What's up?" Alexis said as she walked in. All three of us stared at her as she walked in and dropped her Gucci purse in a chair.

I looked at Alexis, unsure of what I should say. She must've read the look on my face because she crossed her arms across her chest and rolled her eyes. "I guess you told them."

"You guessed right," I replied. All four of us had grown tight over the past year so Alexis had to know that I was going to tell Camille and Angel.

"So? It's no big deal anyway," Alexis said as she took a seat.

"So it's true?" Angel said, walking over to Alexis.

"It's not as serious as I'm sure Jasmine made it out to be." Alexis cut her eyes at me.

"Alexis, what's going on?" Camille said, sitting down next to her.

Alexis broke out into a huge smile. "Trina and I have this cool business going on. She and her cousin get the stuff and then we sell it out of my house."

"So you *are* selling the stuff?" I threw my hands up in disgust. "That's just great."

Alexis ignored me and looked at Camille. "See, the stores all have insurance that replaces the lost stuff so it's not like it's hurting them."

Before Camille could respond, our group leader, Rachel Adams, walked in. She was the first lady of Zion Hill and the founder of Good Girlz. The room grew silent when she entered.

"Don't stop talking on my account," Rachel said as she eyed all of us suspiciously. "You all want to tell me what you're talking about that you don't want me to know?"

We looked at one another. Part of me really wanted to tell Rachel what we were talking about. Maybe she could talk some sense into Alexis. But, of course, I didn't want to sell out my friend like that.

"We were just discussing community service project ideas," Alexis said. I stared at her. I couldn't believe she was sitting up in church lying to the first lady.

Rachel gave us a sly smile as she walked to the front of

the room. "Sure you were. But since you say you're on the subject of community service projects, let's hear some of them."

I sat down as well. We spent the next hour going over ideas but my mind was everywhere but in that room. I knew I was wrong, but I sure was glad when Rachel started praying because that meant we were about to wrap up the meeting. I was anxious to try to talk some sense into these girls. They were from these prissy worlds and just didn't understand the kind of trouble they were setting themselves up for.

After Rachel dismissed us, Alexis dang near broke her neck trying to get outside. I caught up with her at the car, where she was leaning over whispering to Camille and Angel.

"Okay, Trina wants to meet us at my house at nine. She had to go to the wake of a great aunt, that's why she's not here tonight. But she still wanted us to get together tonight so we could open for business tomorrow because the First Ladies are having a slumber party and they've all promised to come by." Alexis talked like she was brokering some million-dollar deal. I stood just outside their little circle with my arms crossed.

"What?" Alexis said when she finally noticed me. "Don't start, Jasmine."

"I just can't believe you," I said. "I mean, how did you even get caught up in something like this?"

"For your information, Miss Goody Two-shoes, Trina's cousin hooked her up, then she had me just helping her out. It's not that serious."

"If you get the stuff from her cousin, why y'all out lifting stuff?" I asked.

"What, are you the police now?" Alexis replied. I knew

she was getting agitated but I didn't care. "Fine," she huffed. "If you must know, we don't usually take the stuff ourselves. Trina just started getting some special requests for outfits, so she came up with the idea to open our own little business and pick up some stuff ourselves. Is that answer good enough for you?"

I couldn't do anything but shake my head.

"Dang, Jasmine. You act like we're taking stuff from you," Alexis said. Finally, she threw her hands up and turned back to Camille.

"You still coming?" Alexis said.

Camille was standing there looking all bug-eyed. It was obvious both she and Angel were excited. "What kind of stuff do you have?" Camille wanted to know.

"Trina got some of everything, girl."

"So, she just walks in and takes the stuff off the rack?" Angel whispered.

"Let's not get into how she got it. All that matters is she got it. Now, if you all want in, let me know."

"Oh, I can't steal anything. Angelica needs me and I can't take the risk of going to jail," Angel said, referring to her six-month-old baby girl.

"And you know I did a week in juvie. Me and jail don't get along," Camille added.

I couldn't believe Camille was even thinking about anything that could get her in trouble. After her boyfriend broke out of jail, didn't tell her he broke out, and convinced her to hide him at her grandmother's house, she'd been arrested. Camille almost lost her mind, but the judge told her she didn't have to go to jail as long as she took part in the Good Girlz group.

"No one's going to jail," Alexis said, rolling her eyes at me. "For some reason Trina gets off on taking the stuff.

And she only does that occasionally. Her cousin usually gets all the stuff. All she wants us to do is get the customers in and store the merchandise because her mother is so nosy."

"Is that all she wants?" I snapped. "Alexis, this is crazy. You're freakin' loaded. Why are you doing this?"

Alexis ignored me and kept talking. "Camille, why don't you guys just come by and check it out? If you're game, you can help us sort the stuff. And hey, maybe even pick up a thing or two for yourselves."

Angel pulled up Camille's arm and looked at her watch. "I really have to be getting home. My mom is with Angelica and she has to go to work at ten."

"How's your mom with the baby?" Alexis asked.

I knew she was trying to get attention off of herself by asking about Angel's relationship with her mom, which had been shaky because Angel had gotten pregnant at fifteen.

"Nah, she's cool now," Angel said. "She's really come around and she loves Angelica. But she was serious when she said I wasn't gon' run the streets. She totally trips if I leave Angelica with her too long."

"I bet she'd trip even more if she knew you were off stealing clothes," I said, shaking my head.

"I'm not even trying to hear you," Alexis said as she turned to Camille. "Are you coming or not?"

"Hey, why not?" Camille shrugged.

I looked at her. "I don't believe you."

"I'm just going to look and see what kind of stuff they got," she responded.

"Whatever." I threw my hands up just as my grandmother pulled into the parking lot. "Just let me know when visiting days are." I shook my head as I climbed in my grandmother's car. I could see they were gon' have to learn the hard way.

Looking for more *inspirational* entertainment *with values*

Don't miss these stories by your favorite authors!

#1 Essence bestselling author ReShonda Tate Billingsley

My Brother's Keeper
After a family tragedy, a young woman learns to forgive in order to find the strength to move on...

Let the Church Say Amen
A reverend's devoted wife works to unite a family torn apart by secrets—and helps her husband understand his family is as important as his congregation.

I Know I've Been Changed
Raedella Rollins ditched her hometown—and her family—to become a famous TV journalist. But she soon discovers that family is the only thing that *truly* matters...

Have a Little Faith
National bestselling author Jacuelin Thomas headlines this heartwarming anthology featuring unforgettable stories about faith, family, and forgiveness. Also includes stories by ReShonda Tate Billingsley, Sandra Kitt, and J.D. Mason.

Available wherever books are sold or at www.simonsays.com.

POCKET BOOKS
A Division of Simon & Schuster
A CBS COMPANY

15652